Penguin Books

A Nail on the Head

Clare Boylan has been a jo...
worked for radio and televisi...
She is well established as a...
appeared in magazines in England, America, Denmark, Australia,
Sweden, South Africa and Norway, and in anthologies such as
Winter's Tales. She has also written a novel, *Holy Pictures*, which was
published by Penguin in 1984. Clare Boylan lives in Wicklow with her
journalist husband and three cats.

Holy Pictures won Clare Boylan considerable critical acclaim: the
Sunday Telegraph wrote, 'an original and mature talent ... here is
an imagination that transmutes reality into the stuff of magic'; *The
Times Literary Supplement* commented, '*Holy Pictures* is a sensitive,
precise and evocative novel ... Clare Boylan's pared-down prose
tantalizingly emphasizes the possibility of a richer, if secret, potential';
and the *Listener* said, 'A sense of humour and a flair for the *mot
juste* are the tools with which Clare Boylan fashions her extravagantly
Irish, extremely funny comedy of manners and madness.'

Clare Boylan

A Nail on the Head

Penguin Books

Penguin Books Ltd, Harmondsworth, Middlesex, England
Viking Penguin Inc., 40 West 23rd Street, New York, New York 10010, U.S.A.
Penguin Books Australia Ltd, Ringwood, Victoria, Australia
Penguin Books Canada Ltd, 2801 John Street, Markham, Ontario, Canada L3R 1B4
Penguin Books (N.Z.) Ltd, 182–190 Wairau Road, Auckland 10, New Zealand

First published in Great Britain by Hamish Hamilton Ltd 1983
Published in Penguin Books 1985

Made and printed in Great Britain by
Richard Clay (The Chaucer Press) Ltd,
Bungay, Suffolk
Filmset in 10/12 Monophoto Sabon by
Northumberland Press Ltd, Gateshead

For My Mother

Contents

Housekeeper's Cut   9

The Wronged Wife   27

Bad-natured Dog   37

Appearances   50

Some Retired Ladies on a Tour   64

Ears   82

Married   90

A Reproduction   97

Not a Recommended Hobby for a Housewife   104

A Nail on the Head   111

Black Ice   127

For Your Own Bad   145

Mama   152

The Complete Angler   164

The Cage   175

Housekeeper's Cut

Edward kept looking into the refrigerator. It gave him a sense of faith. This peculiar sensation billowed inside his chest in the manner competently wrought by carol singers and card senders at Christmas. It was not the same as religious faith. Edward was too modest for that. He was experiencing another sensation never before aspired to in his life, a faith in ordinary things.

There was butter and bacon, eggs, milk, ice-cream; a clutter of untidy vegetables – carrots, cabbage, onions, mushrooms. He had purchased them recklessly from a stall in a food market, cramming his string bag with scabby-looking roots with the air of a man who knows exactly what he is doing. He had no notion of any practical application for such primitive nutrients. They might have been employed by men who lived in caves to club their enemies. He was familiar with food that came in plastic bags and could be persuaded, with boiling water, to imitate a meal.

He knew, all the same, in the way a blind man knows that the world over his head is blue and grey and the world under his feet is green and grey and the top part is safer, that these items belonged at the very heart of things and that this was where he was going.

The thing that pleased him most was his roast. It held the centre of the refrigerator, lightly covered in butcher's paper. He had watched it in the meaty window for several minutes before striding in and claiming it. He did this by pointing because he had no idea what it was. He was appalled at the price. It cost over four pounds. He was neither poor nor mean, merely accustomed to buying a slice or two of roast beef from the delicatessen or a couple of spiced sausages, and there was always plenty of change left over from a pound. Now that it was his he could see that it was worth the money, swirling fat and flesh tied with a string in the middle; already he could hear the clash of knives being sharpened, the rattle and scrape of plates, like sounds of battle imagined by a child in a history class.

He used to meet Susan between meals. She was worn out from making excuses and he had to give her glasses of wine to make her look the way he imagined her when she was not there. She grumbled about the needs of her children, the demands of her husband, his capacity for chops and potatoes and apple tarts. It appeared that her whole life was dragged down by the weight of her husband's appetite; she was up at dawn wringing the vitamins from oranges, out hampered by enormous sacks of groceries during the day. Afternoons were taken up with peeling and grating, marinating, sieving. After a time her abused features would soften and she would say: 'It would be different if it was for you. I always think of that when I'm cooking. I always pretend it's for you.' She would come to him then, dipping her face to his lips. She sat across his legs as if he was a see-saw. 'If you were with me,' he would say, 'I would give you six months of tremendous spoiling. Then I'd put you to work.'

Sometimes he did, just to watch her, just for fun. He put her beside the cooker with mushrooms and cream, small morsels of fish, tasty things.

She was too tired. The food got burnt, the mushrooms went rubbery. Or they became distracted. He would come up behind her and put his arms around her and she would swivel round and burrow to him. When they were in bed smells of burning food and sounds of music drifted up from rooms below.

Inside her, he found a love that wanted to be taken advantage of and although he did not wish to hurt her, he found himself complaining about the comfortlessness of his life; the meals taken in restaurants with people who meant nothing, just to fill an evening. He dined out most evenings because he was lonely in the house without her. She never asked about his companions, but about the interior features of the restaurants, the designs on menus and then in detail, the meal. 'It's a waste,' he said, 'to be anywhere without you.'

When he went back to the city he forgot about her. There were moments when he felt a hollowness which he recognized as the place in him where she had been, but he had always known it would come to an end. He looked on love as a seasonal pleasure, like sunshine. Only a savage expected the sun to shine all year round.

She telephoned from public call boxes. Her voice was the ocean in a seashell. He remembered that they had made together a splash of happiness on a pale canvas but he knew that she did not carry this glow alone, without him. When they said goodbye for the last time, he had watched her running away, a drooping figure, disarrayed, a spirit fleeing an exorcism. He listened to the cascade of coins following the operator's instructions and then after a pause, her weary voice. 'I miss you.' He saw her in a headscarf with a bag of groceries at her side and small children clawing on the outside of the glass, trying to get at her.

He was at home now, busy, surrounded by people who were skilled in the pleasures of living – conversation and lovemaking – as people in the country had never been.

Even she, to whom he had leapt as determinedly as a salmon, held within her a soft hopelessness which begged, come in to me, fill me up, I have nothing else.

One day on the phone her voice sounded different: 'I'm coming up,' she said. He frowned into the machine receiving the bubbles of her tone. This possibility had not occurred to him. She was too firmly anchored with groceries. 'Two whole days,' she was telling him through her laughter, gasping about excuses and arrangements so complicated that he knew she would tunnel under the earth with her hands to reach him if necessary. 'That will be very nice,' he said inadequately. 'I'll look forward to that.' It was when he had replaced the receiver and was still washed by echoes of her foolish joy that he understood properly what she was saying. She had disposed, for a time, of all the open mouths that gaped at her for sustenance. She had put them aside. She was coming to do her proper task. He was tenderly agitated by the thought of her frail figure scurrying from one area of usefulness to another. This was blotted out by the shouts of his own areas of deprivation, crying out to be seen to. He wanted her to look after him.

When he met her at the station she was tremulously dressed up, a country woman on an outing. She threw him a reckless smile from under a hat. Alarming blue carnations sprang up around her skull. She dropped her cases and raced into his arms. Her feet flailed heedlessly and the flowers on her hat dipped like the neck of a heron. She thudded into him and he felt the needy probing of her tongue. He held her patiently, employing his training as a man to grind down the stone in his chest, of disappointment, that she had not kept a part of herself solid and available to his needs.

'Look at that!' She kept stabbing at the window of the car with her gloved finger, demonstrating pigeons and churches and department stores. 'Look!' 'You sound like a tourist,' he said. She kept quiet after that. She hadn't ever been to the city before.

Inside his flat she walked around all the rooms, inspecting his clothes on their hangers, patting the bed, trying out chairs. He was surprised when she sat down without giving a glance to the refrigerator. 'What shall we do?' she said.

She was slouched in a red leather armchair, her white skirt bunched under her thighs. He imagined that she ought to be in the kitchen doing something with the roast. He could picture it bulging in a tin, strung about with peeled potatoes and onions. He wanted to watch her bending at the oven, her frowning face pink, her straight hair shrivelling into tiny curls around her face. He had bought an apron for her. It was white with a black and red frill at the bottom. It hung on a nail by the sink. He had no clear idea of what they would do with all the time they now had to spend together. She was the one who was married, who was skilled in the sectioning of time. He had vaguely imagined that women liked to be busy in a house, arranging flowers, punching pastry, stirring at saucepans on the stove, and that it was a man's role to encircle this ritual with refinement, music and drinks and occasional kisses, creating a territory for their contentment, a privacy for their love.

He had not set his heart on this course of events. He did not mind if she preferred to take a nap or read a book or sit on his knee. The thing that was foremost in his mind was that their pursuits of the afternoon would be overlaid by ovenly aromas, snaps and splutterings and the delicious sting on their senses of roasting meat.

He asked if she was hungry and she said that she was, standing up instantly, brushing down her skirt. She took a mirror from her bag and gazed at her face, pressing her lips together, peering into her eyes for flaws. He took her hand and led her through to the kitchen. He pulled open the door of the refrigerator as if he was drawing back a stage curtain and she peered, awed, at the overcrowding of nourishment. 'What are you going to do with all this?' she said, and he laughed. 'There's cold meat and cheese,' he said. 'We could have that for lunch.' She stood gazing into the fridge with a melancholy expression while he removed the slices of ham and the tubs of potato salad and the oozing triangle of Brie.

When he had set the table and opened a bottle of wine he came back to find her still transfixed in front of the open cabinet with that expression housewives have, and he thought she was sizing up the contents, planning menus. 'That,' he said, pointing in at his slab of meat on the shelf as if it was a lovely trinket in a jeweller's window, 'is for dinner.' She sat down at the table without a word. He sensed, as she ate her ham and potatoes and swirled her wine around in the glass, that she was disappointed. This feeling communicated to himself and he poured wine into his leaden chest, blaming himself. He had probably pre-empted her plans for lunch. She might have been planning to surprise him with a home-made soup. She raised bleak eyes to him over her glass. She was not her normal self, full of cheerful complaint and breath-less love. She was ill at ease and sad. 'Aren't we going out?' she said. The thought to him was preposterous. Now that they finally had a stretch of privacy, she wanted to race out into the cold where they would be divided by elements and the curious looks of strangers.

He drove her to a park and they huddled under some trees against the cold, watching cricket players and a family of deer in the distance like an arrangement of dead branches. He had brought a box of sweets that she had sent him. It had seemed a sentimental gesture, saving them to share with her. Now that he was pulling off the wrapper he could see it was tactless, taking them out so much later. She would think he had not wanted them. He laid the open box in the grass. After a moment or two, the arrangement of confec-tionery was swarming with ants.

He was tired when he got home and beginning to get hungry. Susan wanted a bath. He took the meat from the fridge and laid it on a plate on the counter. He hazarded the skinning of several potatoes. He carried a clutch of jaundiced-looking parsnips and placed them in a bowl, close to the liquidizer. This tableau was completed with a blue tin of curry powder. Once, in a restaurant, he had been given a curried parsnip soup and it was delicious.

When she joined him in the kitchen she was wearing a black dress down to her feet. Her mouth was obscured in magenta. He put his arms around her and kissed her laundered neck but she struggled from his grasp and pointed to the ranked ingredients. 'What are you doing?' she said. 'Just hamming.' He smiled guiltily.

She looked from him to the food, back again. Her hands, he noticed, wrestled with the string of a tiny evening bag. 'I thought,' she said, 'that we'd be going out.' 'Going where?' he said, exasperated. 'I don't know.' Her shoulders drooped. 'The theatre, a restaurant.' He could not keep her still, draw her back to the things that mattered. 'Do you really want to go out?' She nodded her head. He sighed and went to telephone a theatre. When he came back the counter had been cleared of his work and offered instead a meagre plate of toast and a pot of tea.

In the city she was happy. She sipped cocktails and laughed, showing all her teeth, raising her eyebrows larkily. Although her clothes were not suited to the theatre, not suited to anything really, she carried her happiness with dignity. Men looked at her, old ones, young ones, brown, grey. She was aware of this but her eyes were for him. He thought he understood now. She was sure of herself on this neutral territory. She did not wish to be plucked by him from their complicated past. Here, she was a woman alone. She wanted him to court her. He took her hand and kissed her cheek, catching scents of gin and perfume. He felt desire. This seizure of lust was new. It had not touched him when they were in the park or shut up in his living quarters. He had felt love and compassion but no selfish stirrings.

During the play he watched her, writing his own theme, making her free and carefree as his needs required, as her loud laughter would lead anyone to believe.

Afterwards he turned the car quickly homeward. She kept looking out the window, like a child. When they were home

15

she said fretfully: 'We haven't had anything to eat, not really.'
He was no longer concerned about food. There was plenty,
in any case, in the fridge. She cooked some eggs and a packet
of little onions, frozen in sauce. It was a strange combination
but he drove the food into his mouth and pronounced it
delicious.

They went to bed. Their sex was full of need and passion.
They came with angry shouts. They could not find their love.
'I love you,' she said. 'Yes,' he said. 'Yes.' And then they
were silent, each saying to themselves: 'Tomorrow will be
different.'

In the morning she was up early to make his breakfast,
her toes crackling with joy as she reached up to shelves for
coffee and marmalade. She felt wrapped around him as a
cardigan. As she waited for the coffee to boil she sensed a
warm splash on her feet and it was his seed, languorously
detaching itself from her. She felt a minute sense of loss,
wanting to let nothing go, wanting to be pregnant.

Edward had to work after breakfast. He did not mind
leaving her on her own. She seemed happy as she punished
pillows and washed out the breakfast things. He found himself
whistling as he bent over his set square. After a time she
came and sat beside him. She had been washing her hair. She
combed it over her face in long strokes that emanated a faint
creak. Inky streamers swam through the air and clung to his
clothing. He could not work. He gave her an irritated glance
and she went away. She came back dressed in high shoes and
a blue suit – a costume, rather, he thought – her face matt
and piqued with make-up. She was carrying cups of coffee.
When she put his coffee down she quickly sought his hand
with hers, and although their grasp was warm and steady
there was some central part of them that was trembling and
they could feel it through their palms. 'Now,' he thought,
'we could go to bed. We could love each other.' It made

sense. They had always done their loving in the day. Her bright armour kept him distant.

'I'd like,' she said, 'to see the sights.'

He took his hand away and wrapped it around the cup of coffee, needing warmth. He did not look at her. 'There's nothing to see out there,' he said. 'Believe me. We could have a quiet lunch and listen to some music. We could read to each other.' 'But it's London!' she protested.

He said, thinking to stop her: 'You go if you want. I must work for a little while. I couldn't bear to see the sights.' He did look up then and saw her soft round face boxing up a huge hurt in an even larger resolve. She kissed the side of his face and he wanted the salt of her mouth but she was so different, so devoid of humour and generosity, that he believed even her taste might have changed. She clopped off on her high heels and he heard the sorrowful bang of the door.

He could not work. He was exasperated to distraction. There crept in on him thoughts, malice-filled whispers. He shook them off as if they were wasps at his ears.

He had established in his mind, long months before, that she was the one in his life who truly loved him, wanting nothing, knowing that nothing was possible. When they parted he had savoured the sorrow of it, knowing that this was real. They had been severed by fate, an outsider, a true professional. There would be no festering, only a clean grief gleaming like stainless steel around the core of a perfect happiness, safely invested in his centre. He had been content to leave it at that. He would have loved her, at the back of his head, until his death.

It was she who had come back like a vengeful spirit to incorporate him in her discontent, to mock his faith, to demonstrate to him, in her ghostly unreachableness, the great stretch of his own isolation.

He went to look for some lunch. There was nothing in the

refrigerator that he could understand. He was exploring parcels of foil, hoping for some forgotten cheese, when he heard a commotion coming from the garden.

Susan was in a restaurant. She had a chocolate éclair that she was breaking with the side of her fork. She had taken a taxi to Madame Tussaud's and the Planetarium. Outside each was a long queue of foreigners and a man selling balloons on a stick for fifty pence. There was no glamour, no sense of discovery. They were like people queueing for food in the war. She had wanted him to take her to a gallery of famous paintings and show her the pictures he liked. No point in going on her own; she could never understand pictures, always wanted to see the scene as it really was.

She left the stoic queue and went back to the taxi rank. She could not think where to go. 'Bond Street,' she said to the driver, liking its sound. She did not know where it was but it seemed to her, as the streets unravelled like red and grey bandages, she was being taken further and further away from Edward. When they got to Bond Street, she was ordered out of the dark enclosure. She tried to thrust a fan of notes at the back of the driver's neck, through the sliding glass door, but he was suspicious and made her go out on the street and put them through a side window.

She stumbled along in front of the smart shops. She ached to be with Edward, to feel his hand or even the cloth of his jacket; and then, perversely, she felt lonely for home, wanting to butter toast for the children or to fluff the top of a shepherd's pie for her husband. She understood their needs. She knew how to respond. When she had exhausted several streets she found a café and she went in and ordered herself a cake. A tear dropped into it and she did not want to eat it. She would go back, she promised herself. She would talk to him.

He was standing at the window, shoulders bent, head at

a quizzical angle and sunlight teasing his hair into infantile transparency. She had let herself in with the key he had given her and he did not notice her. Watching his back, she felt as if all the ordinary things had been vacuumed out of her body and replaced by love, lead-heavy, a burden. 'I want to talk to you,' she said. 'Shhh,' he said, not turning around. 'Edward?' she begged. He turned to her. His face was white, filled with horror. 'It's a bird,' he said.

'What are you talking about?' She went to the window and looked out. She could see a ragged tomcat standing at a tree, his back arched. She ran to the back door and out into the garden, down the length of the path.

The tree was root deep in rattling leaves and when she got to it she could see that the leaves were in permanent motion as if agitated by a slow motor under the earth. She saw then that it was a dowdy grey bird, lopsided, helplessly urging an injured wing to flight. The cat held its victim with a goose-berry gaze. She picked up the cat and put it on the wall, slapping its behind to make it jump into the next garden. 'Bring me a box,' she shouted out to Edward's white face at the window. He advanced with a shoe box. She snatched it from him, piling it with leaves, roughly cramming in the damaged bird. She slammed the lid on the bird's head and carried it indoors. She looked, Edward thought, like a house-wife who has just come upon some unpleasant item of refuse and means to deal with it; but when she got indoors she sat in a chair and emptied bird and leaves into her blue linen lap. She held the bird in cupped hands and crooned gently into its dank feathers.

He brought her tea and fed it to her, holding the cup to her mouth. She minded the bird like a baby, making noises with her lips, rocking back and forth as once she had minded him. He was unnerved by a pang of jealousy. 'Did you have a nice morning?' he said. 'Oh, yes,' she said, distantly, rocking. He could see that she was in her element. He was excluded.

He crumbled bread into a bowl of milk and pushed little spoons of it at the dry nib of the bird's beak. The bird seemed to be asleep. She pushed his hand aside and swept the bird, leaves and all, back into the box. 'Open the bedroom window,' she said. She followed him upstairs and put the box on the ledge without its lid. 'If his wing isn't broken he'll fly away,' she said. 'But if it is broken?' he said helplessly. 'He'll die,' she said.

In the course of the morning he had taken the meat and vegetables from the fridge once more. There had been nothing readily edible and he was hungry. When they came downstairs again she saw them and said: 'I have to phone my husband,' as if they had reminded her of him, which they had.

He heard her on the phone. She sounded as if she was defending herself. She said then: 'I miss you.' It was an echo from his distant past. He went in and found her sitting on the sofa, her fist to her mouth, crying. He touched her hair lightly with his fingers, afraid to do more. 'I'll just put the meat in the oven,' he said hopefully. 'What?' She glared at him. Her tearful face was full of scorn. 'Have you still got your heart set on that?' 'I bought it for you,' he said. 'You bought it for me? I have tasted prawns and sole in my life, you know. I have had fried steak.' She was attacking him. He didn't know what was the matter. He assumed her husband had said something to upset her. 'It's all right,' he soothed. He tiptoed out as if she were sleeping.

The potatoes, peeled from yesterday, had blackened. He flung them hopefully into the tin. He peeled four onions and tucked them into the corners; in the centre, as he had imagined it, the round of juicy meat.

It looked perfectly fine. He put a pat of butter on the top and a sprinkling of salt and pepper. He cut up a clove of garlic and scattered it over the food. He thought he had seen other women doing something like this. He turned the oven up to a rousing temperature and pushed the tin inside. It was done. There was nothing to it.

He blamed himself for Susan's outburst. He should not have left her to wander around the city on her own. She was used to a more protected way of life. He must make it up to her.

He took champagne from a cool cupboard and dug it into a bowl with ice. He found music on the radio. He brought the wine with glasses to the bedroom. Music drifted up from downstairs. He drew the curtains and switched on a little lamp. 'Susan,' he called.

He heard her dragging steps on the stairs. A face loomed round the door, self-piteous. Her sharp eyes flashed about suspiciously, took in the details – and were radiant. She was a child; all troubles erased in a momentary delight. She ran to him and was caught in his arms. They stroked hair, pulled buttons, tasted flesh. She laughed greedily. At last they had met.

They made love boastfully, tenderly, certain of their territory. He held her feet in his hands. She took his fingers in her mouth. They embroidered one another's limbs with their attentions. He felt with his lips for the edges of her smile and could find no end. They were separated only by the selfishness of their happiness. Afterwards, she gave a deep unlikely chortle from her satisfied depths and he laughed at her.

They drank the champagne crouching at opposite ends of the bed in the intimate gloom, striking up flinty tales of childhood for sympathy.

When they crawled towards each other, he with bottle and she with empty glass, only their mouths met and he took the breakable things and put them on the floor because they had to make love again.

They emptied the bottle of champagne. They lay beside each other, gazing. 'I must look awful,' she said. He surveyed her snarled black hair and the matching dark scribble under a carelessly disposed arm; the smear of make-up under her eyes, her sated face scrubbed pink. 'You look fine to me,' he said. He felt exuberant, relieved, re-born, at ease. 'You look,' he teased, but truthfully, 'like my mistress.'

She swung away from him, rolled over and clung to her pillow, a mollusc on a rock. He could not tell what was in her head. He patted her back but she shook him off and murmured sadly through the pillow: 'I smell something.' She looked up at him, one moist eye rising above its ruined decor. He had offended her. But when the rest of her face rose above the sheets he could see that her eyes were watering with laughter.

'What is it?' he smiled tenderly. 'It's perfect,' she said. 'It's exactly as it used to be – us, together, the music and the smell of burning food.' She laughed.

He jumped out of bed and ran to the kitchen. Smoke gusted out around the oven door. The air was cruel with the taint of burning beast. He pulled open the oven door and his naked body was assaulted by the heat of hell. He dragged the roasting tin clear of the smoke with a cloth. The cloves of garlic rattled like blackened nails on the tarry ruin.

He was worn out. He felt betrayed. He could not believe that it had happened so quickly, so catastrophically. He felt his faith sliding away. 'Edward?' Susan called out from the bedroom. 'It's all right!' he shouted; and after he had said it he felt that it had to be. He opened the window to let out the smoke and went to the bathroom for a dressing-gown.

Bolstered by champagne and the satisfactoriness of the afternoon's loving he made himself believe that the meat could be repaired. He whistled loudly as if it was the dark and he was afraid. He forked the meat on to a scallopped plate and began to hack away with a sharp knife at the charred edges of the tormented flesh.

He was agreeably surprised to find that the meat was still quite rare on the inside – almost raw, in fact. He found it hard to make an impression with the knife but he put this down to lack of practice and the fact that the carving implements were not much in use. He sawed, glad of the little box of cress in the fridge which would decorate its wounds and the rest of the vegetables which Susan would cook and toss in butter while he put on his clothes.

Susan came up behind him. She had been standing in the doorway in a night-dress like a flourbag, frilled on cuff and sleeve. She tiptoed on bare feet, so that he sensed her at the last moment, tangled wraith blanched and billowing.

'It's no use,' she whispered. 'It's fine,' he said. 'It's not bad at all.' 'It's no use,' she cried brokenly. 'There's no Bisto, no stock cubes. There's nothing in your cupboards, nothing ordinary – no flour or custard, there isn't a packet of salt. It's all a pretence.'

She put out a hand, and he reached for it, needing something to hold. Her hand shot past him. She struck at the meat. It sailed off the plate and landed on the floor, blood gathering at its edges. 'That's all you think of me,' she said violently, through trembling jaws. 'You think that's good enough for me! Housekeeper's Cut! I wouldn't have that on my own table at home. I wouldn't give that to my children if they were hungry. That's all I'm worth.'

They ate in an Italian restaurant close to where he lived. It was not a place he had been before. The tables were bright red and the menu leaned heavily to starch but there was no time to book a proper restaurant. He had to have something to eat.

'Have some veal,' he said. 'That should be good.' He poured wine from a carafe into their glasses. She ordered a pizza. Her hair fell over her face. He could see her knuckles sawing over the fizzing red disc but none of it seemed to go to her mouth. The waiter said that the lady should have an ice-cream. She shook her head. 'Cassata!' he proclaimed. 'It means,' he wheedled, '*married*.'

Edward laughed encouragement but she did not see. Her head was turned to the waiter, nodding, he could not tell whether in request or resignation.

In the morning she was gone. The sheets still burned with the heat of her body. She had been up at six, packing, making coffee, telephoning for a taxi. Her feet, on the floor made a rousing slap like the sound of clapping hands. At one point he heard her whistling. He knew that he should drive her to the station but he would not hasten her back to the disposal of her lawful dependants. He would not.

'Edward!' Her hands clung to the end of his bed and she cried out in distress, her face and her night-dress trailing white in the grey morning light. 'Yes, love,' he said inside, but he only opened a cautious eye and uttered a sleepy 'Mmm?' 'I bought nothing for the children,' she said. 'They'll be expecting presents. I always buy them something.'

She stood at the window, dressed in hat and coat, in the last moments, waiting for her taxi. 'Edward!' she cried. He sat up this time, ready to take her in his arms. 'The bird!' she said. 'He flew away.'

When she was gone he traced with his fingers her body in the warm sheets, bones and hair and pillows of maternal flesh. He kept his eyes closed, kept her clenched in his heart. The day bore in on him, sunshine and telephone bells and the cold knowledge that she did not love him. All the time she pretended to care for him, she had been jealous of his wealth, greedy for glamour. She was a pilgrim, stealing relics of the saints.

It was not him she desired. She wanted to snatch for herself some part of a glittering life she imagined he was hoarding. He tried to bring her face to mind but all he could see was a glass box, clawed by children, and inside, a housewife in a headscarf, bags of groceries at her side.

Susan did not cry until she was on the train. The tears fell, then, big as melted ice cubes. There was a man sitting opposite with a little boy. The child had been given a magic drawing pad to occupy his hands and he made sketches of her melting face, squinting for perspective.

As the tears dashed from her eyes she felt that she was flying to pieces. Soon there would be nothing left of her; at any rate, nothing solid enough to contain the knowledge that he did not love her.

She had expected so little. She only wanted to fill up the gaps in their past. Often, when they were together, he had spoken of the hurt of being anywhere without her; the wasted nights with strangers; the meals in restaurants, not tasted. It was terrible to her that she had only given him her leftover time. She had to make it up to him. She wanted him to know that she would risk anything for him. She would shine beside him in the harsh glare of public envy. For a very little time she would be his for all the world to see, whatever the world might say.

Now she did not know what she would do except, in time, face up to her foolishness. He had not been proud of her. He wanted to hide her away. Established in his own smart and secret life, he had been ashamed of her.

The man on the seat opposite was embarrassed. It was her huge tears, her lack of discretion, the critical attention of his little boy. He felt threatened by their indifference to proper codes of behaviour. He snatched the magic pad and threw it roughly to the far end of the seat. The boy gazed idly out the window.

Accustomed to inspecting the creative efforts of the children, Susan reached for the sketch pad. The boy was not as clever as her own. His portrait was a clown's mask, upside down. She rubbed out his imprint and sat with the pad on her knee, acquainting herself with the raw, hurting feeling of her mind and her skin, settling into the pain. She had to

25

stop crying. The children would notice. Tomorrow she would buy them presents. Tonight, they would have to content themselves with ice-cream. 'Ice-cream' she scratched absently on the magic pad. Her tired mind grizzled over the necessities of tea and she wrote, without thinking, 'eggs, bacon, cheese'; and then, since days did not exist on their own but merely as transport to other days, and since she on this vehicle of time was a stoker, she continued writing: 'carrots, cabbage, onions, mushrooms'.

The Wronged Wife

'My wife would like to meet you,' Matthew said one day when she was gazing out the window at a stubble of bluebells wobbling in the breeze.

'I am your wife,' Vanessa said. 'I've met myself.' She turned to look into eyes that were blue and wobbled with the same charming uncertainty as the flowers. 'Margaret,' he specified. 'Oh, that wife,' she smiled, coming over to rub his hair in the hope that he would clasp his hands around her bottom, and he did.

She was disturbed. Getting Matthew through his divorce had been like setting a person's house on fire and then rescuing them from the blaze. She woke each morning like a child at Christmas, afraid to open her eyes in case the gift was not there. She still held her breath in awe at the precious bulk in the blankets and felt faint with pride when he called her name in the evenings as he stepped into the hall.

She had not unpacked all her clothes for fear of intruding too massively on his wardrobe.

When she first came to the house there were traces of Margaret. It was a perfume, an atmosphere. The place was meticulously clean, cleaner than any place she had ever been in. So remorselessly had it been polished that it was weeks before she had anything to do. She passed her days in opening spotless cupboards searching for Margaret. And there she was; in the lists that had been pasted up on the insides of the doors, specifying the correct contents of each cupboard so that replacements could be made before they became necessary; in the curious military ranking of drinking glasses and bottles which suggested that she was not aware they had any pleasure to offer her other than the arranging of them; in the set of silver cutlery which she disturbed from its gleaming repose on a bed of black velvet. The reverence with which each piece had been prepared and put away in order of size reminded her of a family mortuary. There was merit in the assembly. You could tell at a glance if anything was missing. All the same, anyone else would have just flung them in in a bundle with egg between the prongs.

Her first instinct was to rip down the lists and sully a good glass with whisky to celebrate. She found it was not possible. The lists were useful. It seemed wanton to destroy them unless she had something better to contribute. She hadn't. She was still considering her situation when her own untidiness caught up with her. Webs and dust and little heaps of articles of daily usage sprang up around her. She swept and wiped and sorted in a panic. Matthew was not critical. He kissed her and helped with the housework in a useless, endearing manner. He reminded her that Margaret had been keeping house for a dozen years, that Rome wasn't built in a day. He was endlessly tactful and patient. She underdid his egg and overdid his beef and he said nothing for months. When he was driven to instruct her on his preferences he added: 'It was years before Margaret got that right.'

Already she was learning that marriages are not, as the law so optimistically offers, dissolved. Men are hoarders. First wives have to be accommodated in some attic of the marriage like an embarrassing Mrs Rochester. With Margaret it was different. There was no reason to think of her as a malign presence. It was her goodness that held them. She remained central, like a piece of mahogany that had to be displayed because it was too good to throw away.

Vanessa was overwhelmed by the uselessness of competing with Margaret but she scrubbed the house so thoroughly it looked sore and converted her misgivings to understanding.

Now and again there were things that surpassed her understanding. Why on earth should Margaret want to come and see her? She had never met Margaret but she knew about her. Matthew had talked of her while they were having their affair. She was thirty-seven which was twelve years more than Vanessa and she had given him the best years of her life. The divorce would kill her. In the harrowing months of legal severance Vanessa had wanted to talk to her. Matthew would not allow it. It was no use trying to be friends with her, he reasoned. She was entitled to her hostility. She frowned over the trampled field of Matthew's hair. 'Why now?' she wondered. He pushed his head between her breasts and joggled them therapeutically. 'Because that's the sort of person she is,' he said. 'She has survived the worst of it and she wants us to know she's all right – so we won't feel guilty.'

As always she knew he was right. She still didn't like the idea. She wanted her guilt. It had come in a parcel with her new life and she felt that she must hold it all or lose it all.

When the day came she opened tender Charentais melons and bathed strawberries in liqueur. She sliced tomatoes and buried them in a flurry of chopped parsley. Matthew popped in to say he was on his way. The divorce had left Margaret without a car and he had to collect her. He stole a slice of tomato and reminisced. In his first marriage there had been a small pot on the kitchen window with a basil plant. It was like a child's drawing of a plant and it grew abundantly although it was constantly snipped and shredded over tomatoes. He had not actually realized that fresh tomatoes had the taste and texture of a handkerchief soaked in sweat until ... 'Must be off. I'll give Margaret a drink on the way home so you'll have time to look beautiful.' 'Oh,' Vanessa called out in distress. 'What does she look like?' 'Battered,' he sighed, lowering his eyebrows as if offended. He kissed her and left her trembling amid the vegetables. She pulled a salad limb from limb. She would make Matthew proud of her. Margaret was coming home. Her pink fingernails shook like the blossoms of hydrangea in a storm and were deluged by a storm of her tears.

When she had cried for half an hour she began to feel better. She could see herself back at work, eating sandwiches in pubs, carrying large paper bags with dresses inside, sitting on the edge of a single bed pulled close to a gas fire, sharing a half bottle of gin with a girlfriend. She felt calmer. She put the potatoes on to boil and made a plain salad – nothing that her shaking hand could mangle or her jealous heart curdle. She bronzed pieces of pork and mushrooms in butter and put them growling in cream.

A girl walked into the kitchen wearing men's boots and a fragile white blouse. She had a cigarette in her mouth. 'Hello, flower,' she said in a small voice. Vanessa stared hard at her in surprise. There were women's lines around her eyes. She wasn't a girl at all. She swung her long hair and stamped over to the cooker in her everyday jeans, the curious effect of girlhood and womanhood superimposed. The girl or woman grinned into the pan, dripping ash on the food. 'Aren't you good?' she said. 'All this stuff.'

Matthew crept up on them and dropped a whisky kiss on Vanessa's ear. 'Margaret – Vanessa,' he presented. The two of them studied each other without reserve. In silence, scarcely disturbed by the hiss of the food in the pan, they made their adjustments. It required great concentration and was necessary for each to become the other, to wind their transposed limbs around the husband and absorb his words of love, to think: she knows he gets dandruff. She knows he can't eat oysters. She knows he whimpers when he comes.

Matthew stood winter limbed, a peripheral hedge to their whirling seasons, until he could stand it no longer and bellowed, 'Sherry, darling?' at Vanessa. 'Yes,' Vanessa said and Margaret said: 'Have a whisky, dear, or you'll never catch up. We're as pissed as newts.'

They went into the drawing room like visitors and sat in its special tidiness. Matthew poured spirits for himself and Margaret and hovered the bottle over a third glass. 'Sure?' He gave Vanessa a last chance. She nodded her head and boldly asked for ice.

She wanted Margaret to know that she had authority with her husband and to understand that she was not irresponsible in the matter of household management. The lavatory gleamed. The ice-box was crammed with long white rocks like Americans' teeth.

'He's a very hard man,' Margaret said when Matthew had left the room. 'He's very sure of himself.' The woman was an imposter, Vanessa decided. 'You don't understand him,' she said carefully. 'Oh, I do,' Margaret said. 'I spent twelve years understanding him. It's what wives do. It's like bloody housework, dear. You break your back crawling under the bed to scrape away heaps of dust that nobody else even knows are there. D'you know the worst of it? It's not really understanding at all. You're weaving the loose threads back into the fabric, trying to make him into the man you promised yourself. It's only when he's gone that you see him quite clearly – quite a different person, quite independent of all your effort. All that work, and for nothing.' She rocked her whisky lovingly. 'Not that I ever did the other.'

'The *other*?' Vanessa gave the word a sinister emphasis.

'Under the bed.'

Matthew returned from the kitchen and hovered in the doorway with the ice bucket, his big ambling body made fragile by uncertainty, his eyes innocent and anxious to please. Vanessa's heart mushroomed with love. He came to sit beside her and plunked two cubes into her drink. He watched her while she tasted it. 'All right, darling?' 'Perfect,' she said, transferring the adjective to his person with her eyes. His expression sharpened for an instant when Margaret threw back her head and dropped the entire measure of whisky down her throat like a frog swallowing a fly. 'I think we ought to eat now,' he said, and Vanessa thought he was right so she left her drink and led them through to the dining room.

The table looked like a holy grotto. The melons were shallow rock pools in the light of two purple candles and a tuft of pious little purple flowers nested in a brandy glass. Each fresh venue imposed its own inhibitions and they became strangers again to scoop their fruit. When Vanessa brought the meat and vegetables from the kitchen Matthew gave her a private lover's smile and brought the purple flowers to his nose. They were hybrids – 'Natureless as a model's armpits', as Margaret predicted. He put them back and gave his attention to the food.

The pork had been transferred to a Provençal casserole and the tomatoes rested on a china dish that was painted with green flowers. Buttered potatoes rose in a glossy mound like a Croque-en-bouche from a platter of thick wood. Matthew was leaning forward. His hands hung between his knees. His eyes were round with longing. 'Poor lamb,' Margaret whispered. It was a tiny sound but it almost caused Vanessa to drop a dish. Matthew had not heard at all. He was hungry. He wanted his dinner. 'Look at him.' Margaret smiled into Vanessa's shocked face. 'They're all our children, men. Small fry. You have to get used to that. It can be a bother when you're young and have been brought up to expect that power and wisdom is a little bulge in a person's trousers. It's an unreliable thing on which to found an empire. Most men would rather have something really useful under their belt, like a torch or a penknife. It's women who have the power. Nobody expects them to do anything and look how much they do. They can never be wrong, only wronged.'

Vanessa was concerned that the food might be cold. She began to spoon it on to plates while Matthew splashed purple wine into glasses. She need not have worried. Matthew was too hungry to notice and Margaret was definitely tight. When

Vanessa passed the dish of tomatoes she extinguished her cigarette on it and handed it back. She herself was unable to eat. She felt ill with shame at something Margaret had said about wronged women. 'Have you been wronged?' she pleaded. 'Oh, yes,' Margaret agreed eagerly. Vanessa shook her head in anguished query. 'And so have you, my dear,' Margaret went on, eating a potato from her fingers. 'Oh, not by the divorce, flower. Oh, no. It's a great freedom to be released from the responsibility of a man. I've got myself a job.' She looked at Matthew. He was twirling a glass of wine in the candlelight, assessing its clarity. 'And a fella.' She went on watching him. He pursed his mouth and fished with the end of his fork for a speck of something in his glass. 'He fancies me. He doesn't look at me with sympathy and tell me I'm tired.' Matthew cornered the foreign body and withdrew it with triumph. He grounded it on a napkin. Margaret's forehead puckered in irritation. She looked away from him and became vague, seeming to forget the route of her thoughts.

'It's this ...' She made a theatrical gesture with her hands over the dinner. 'We ought never to have met. Don't you see, my dear, we've both lost our freedom. I'll feel responsible for you because you're so young and you for me, because I'm not. It was kind of you to insist on my coming here but it was wrong.'

'But I ...' Across the table Matthew was nodding at her like a priest. She assembled the dirty dishes cautiously and carried them to the kitchen. Matthew followed jauntily carrying a pepper pot. 'Let's have some of your marvellous coffee,' he cried out. 'For Christ's sake make it strong,' he hissed when they were alone.

Two bottles of wine had been emptied. They picked the strawberries from intoxicating broth with their fingers while the percolator was burping. Matthew talked to Margaret about money. He wanted to know if she had coped with her tax forms and had she been robbed by the chancer she brought in to do the drains. Margaret answered soberly and smoked cigarettes in rapid succession.

They spoke about children. Vanessa said she wanted a child and Matthew frowned. Margaret said it would make him young again and he smiled. Margaret explained that she had never wanted children but still expected to be stricken by womb panic at thirty-nine when every ball would seem a crystal ball. Matthew frowned. He rose from the table and padded to the corner where he fiddled with some machinery. A flood of music rose from a teak cabinet. He sat with his wives. They raised eyes of shiny emotion to him, blurred in the maudling glow of the candles and it tore at his heart to think that there was only one of him. The music of Schubert had begun upon a single piano as a skipping stream. It had risen to a flood, swirling above their heads, carrying them in its sweetness. Languid and submissive they curved about the table, heads almost touching in the shivering halo of light. No word was spoken until the music found its end. Matthew sprang lightly to his feet, a faint smile touching the corners of his mouth. He rescued the coffee pot and spouted fragrant blackness into two cups. 'None for me,' he exclaimed cheerily. 'For Christ's sake get some into her,' he whispered too loudly, eyeing Margaret, as though it was a decisive move in an important game of cards.

He left them with their coffee to go to the bathroom. The women watched each other over the rim of their cups. 'You're not what I expected,' Vanessa said. 'No,' Margaret said. 'I'm not the person you would picture as Matthew's wife. I tried to be. When I was young I tried. He kept moving the rung up higher. I'm not a good athlete.'

'He's changed,' Vanessa protested. 'He's so good with me. So gentle.'

'Once he did an inventory of all the items in cupboards,' Margaret said. 'He made out little lists and pasted them on the doors of presses. When things ran out he marked a red tick against the item on the list. I felt those red marks as if they had been put on my body with a stick. Whenever I gave myself a drink he would rearrange the bottles afterwards and polish the glasses.'

'The silver spoons?' Vanessa whispered.

'He placed them on a bed of black velvet, like a jeweller's display. It showed up the shine, he said. What he meant was, it emphasized the tarnish. I polished them to please him. "Look!" I said. "It took all day." He threw a hand over his mouth. "Ruined," he said. "You've scratched them all. They're utterly ruined."'

She looked up abruptly. 'You're not happy, are you dear?' Vanessa thought about it. It had not occurred to her that this sodden feeling was unhappiness. She knew that it was love. She had imagined it was happiness. 'It's all right,' Margaret said. 'You don't get extra points for being happy. Happiness is hell, you know. I've been through that too. You're on a peak, looking into the jaws of hell. It's the ultimate despair.'

He returned from the lavatory looking as if he had been on a fortnight's holiday. His hair was full of vigour and he rubbed his hands together, smiling at the women as if he was going to make a meal of them. They regarded him with criticism. 'It's time we got you home,' he beamed at Margaret. 'It's all right,' she said. 'I'll get a taxi.' 'I'll drive you,' he said. 'Vanessa likes me out from under her feet when she's doing the dishes. She insists.' Across the debris of their meal Margaret threw her the ghost of a mischievous glance but she rose from the table quite steadily and went with him like a lamb.

When he got back an hour later the room had gone cold and was wrapped about in its own silence. Vanessa sat on a hard chair nursing the dregs of someone's brandy. He patrolled the room to assess its mood and offered it a chuckle. 'I expect you need that,' he indicated her drink. 'It's been quite an evening.' 'I don't need it,' she said quietly. 'I like it.' 'She's gone to pieces, poor thing,' he said cheerfully. 'But I think the evening did her good.' Vanessa said nothing. He began to be perturbed. 'You're tired,' he diagnosed. 'You've been working hard.'

'Yes,' she said. It had been hard work unpacking all her clothes in an hour and finding homes for them. She had had to dispossess two of his older suits of hangers and put his cashmere sweaters in the linen press. The lists had been stuck up with glue. It needed boiling water and a scrubbing brush to obliterate them. 'All in a good cause,' he said faintly, coming over to put a kiss on her pale forehead. 'Yes,' she said.

He unlaced her fingers from the brandy glass and stepped merrily into the kitchen. He stopped. She counted seconds of silence and predicted exactly the moment when her glass would reach the counter with a tiny note of query.

'It would appear,' he called out, innocently bewildered, 'that the dishes have not been washed.'

As always, he was right.

Bad-natured Dog

The gate was locked and there was a sign saying *bad-natured dog*. There was no bell. She stepped through a gap in the hedge and her large foot mashed a frilly little border of petunias. When she was in the garden she looked up and was momentarily disturbed to see a yellow sponge, squeezed out, moving behind the window, as if someone was washing the glass. The sponge was attached to a blue smocked shirt. It was Levingston, his head waving in bewildered disappointment. He had been spying at the window and thought the person rattling the gate was someone else.

She called out. 'Hi! I'm Nellie Fraser. We talked on the phone.' He stayed where he was, watching her behind the wavy glass. She was tall. She had a mass of brown hair in which there were little sprigs of yellow. She wore pink shorts and a white Indian cotton blouse and even at the distance he could see the brown dots dancing underneath like the bouncing ball that helped you keep time at a sing-along (but that was long ago).

At first the name meant nothing for he was confused by irritation. All the young people who loved the telephone grew accustomed to distant communication and could not be bothered to close even the smallest gap in order to lower their voices. They shouted at you through their noses. He saw that the black shoulder bag she carried was a recording machine. He remembered. She was Nellie Fraser. She was nineteen and she was coming for a scoop.

He made tea while she talked about herself. 'Good thing you don't go into the city,' she shouted from the next room.

'It's a hell of a journey on the train. Five hours, wow. The Orient Express without champagne.' A flurry of innocent laughter came at him like a scarf in the wind. He smiled. She was a pretty thing. 'I know you don't go into the city. *And* I know there isn't a dog. I read it in *The Times*. I've been boning up on you. You haven't given an interview in twenty years. I consider this an honour, you know. I think ...' she paused to make sure he was listening – 'that you are the greatest writer living today.'

With a spoon in one hand, he cowered: that all of his life's work, the good and the bad, the soaring and the waning, the receding tide that made such beguiling clatter over the shingle of a life's experience, should be delivered over to the un-qualified admiration of a big girl of nineteen. He remembered one of the reasons why he had stopped giving interviews.

He had not meant to give this one. When she offered her name on the telephone he thought it was someone else. His hearing was not good any more. He mistook the name. 'Do come up,' he had said with enthusiasm. 'Come as soon as you like.' She told him then about the magazine, the scoop, her big break. He could not put her off without sounding foolish. In the interval between her call and her arrival, he once more foxed himself and put a different name in his diary. Watching her arrival through the window, he had been astonished to note that she was wearing shorts. That was just a moment. It came clear in his head very quickly.

He brought through the tray of tea and saw that she had set up her tape recorder and, as if she trusted the device no more than he did, she had a small notebook balanced on her bare knee.

'Right-o,' he said, turning his back on her to pour the tea. 'Fire away.'

There was a click as she turned on the thing. 'Jasper Levingston,' she said severely. 'You are one of the greatest writers of the century. You are seventy-eight.' She sounded like a policeman about to serve a summons. 'What has been the major influence on your work over three quarters of a century?'

He resisted an urge to chuckle. 'She thinks I started writing when I was three.' He managed to present her with a solemn face and a cup of weak tea. 'Love!' He said.

'Love?' Her amazed voice meandered over several syllables as if he had said bootlaces or bananas. She snapped off the recording machine.

'Come on, Mr Levingston, that's a load of crap,' she said. 'That's the sort of thing pop singers say. Just talk the way you write, with plenty of guts. The magazine is punchy, you know.'

He was drinking his tea. He wished he had brought out a nice biscuit to go with it. The girl, so far as he could tell, had brought nothing. 'My father,' he said, 'did a bit of acting. When he grew old he spent all his time showing off his photographs and little cuttings from the newspapers. Once he acted with Harry Turtle. That meant a lot to him. He used to tell everyone about that. I've never told anyone before.'

'God,' Nellie said. 'Fantastic.' She had furtively switched on the machine again. 'Who was Harry Turtle?'

'I don't know,' Levingston said. 'Father married late. He was my age when I was fourteen, and he was ill. Mother was busy and she used to send me in to sit with him. It was very boring; the tiny paragraphs snipped from provincial newspapers, the rust-coloured photographs – and Harry Turtle.'

'Yeah, well,' Nellie said. 'Old people.' And she looked embarrassed. 'I have a list of questions. Martha in *Sheep's Head* and Georgina in *Woodcut* experience difficulty in climaxing with their men. Is this reverberative of your own experience or is it a symbol for the sexual repression of a generation of women?'

'One day an amazing thing happened. A man called. He

was from the radio and did a sort of looking-back thing once a week. He wanted to put father on the radio. After he had gone, father went into a kind of trance. He sat up in bed clutching his photographs with such a smile on his face. He still told the same stories, but now he prefaced them with: "As I was saying on the radio ..." To mother he would say: "Are we on yet, mother?" and she would give him the date once more. When it was time for the broadcast mother brought an enamel basin into the bedroom and put it on the locker by his bed. She set the wireless beside this and put the headphones in the basin. Only one person could listen on the headphones but if you put them in a basin or a bucket and put your head down, the noise came up at you.

'We were all crouched around the radio and father had my hand in a terrible grip. I was fourteen, an immortal. Father was not content to share his moment. He was sparring with me on my level of dreaming. "Harry Turtle," he said, "acted with me, but he was never on the radio." I turned on him furiously. I could see Harry Turtle forever gesticulating on the path of my life. If I could lay hands on him I would break his bones into sticks and fling them on the fire. "Pox and farts to Harry Turtle," I said. I snatched my hand away and ran from the house.'

He lifted his cup to his mouth but the tea did not go in. It made a pink puddle on the rim of his lip and he sucked several times to blot it away. His eyes were mad with the vividness of remembering.

'I can still recall the feeling I had that day. I felt utterly damned and utterly free. I had no money. I walked into town with my hands in my pockets. There was a motor show-room in the town and I wanted to look at a navy blue open Wolsley that was on display.

'When I got to the street it was filled with the music of a dance band and there were crowds of people about the door of the show-room. A man and a girl danced out into the street in their overcoats. I started to run. It was the most exciting moment of my life. "What is it? What's happening?" I shouted to people who were as full of friendship as if it was New Year's Eve. And a girl, a pretty girl, who was about seventeen and had a fur collar on her coat turned to me with laughing eyes and said: "It's a loudspeaker. It's the first demonstration of the loudspeaker. Isn't it wonderful?" "Wonderful," I shouted. We kept smiling at each other for four or five seconds. She had a very full mouth and I could see the shining pink skin of its inside. I have never responded to anyone so wholly in my life.'

The girl had a petulant look, her jaw stuck out, her bare legs spread, like a child left sitting too long on its pot. 'It just came into my head,' he said. Her notebook was empty. 'You said something about love,' she remembered.

'Yes.'

There was silence until Nellie Fraser could not endure it, and said: 'Love is all shit. It's the universal cop-out. "I lived for love", "I died for love". Balls! I never met a man who didn't have sex on his mind when he talked about love but the pigshit hypocrites won't even admit it. I thought you'd be different, you know.' She shook her pencil at him reproachfully. 'You'd like to go to bed with me, wouldn't you?'

He approximated a wry look of chivalry.

'Aw, come on. Wouldn't you?'

Extraordinary. The notion had not crossed his head. When he had seen the brown dots of her nipples dancing beneath her blouse the thing he thought was that young people never felt the cold. The remembrance of young girls' bodies still nested in his limbs as did the feeling of sitting in the top of a tree when he was a boy of six or seven but he had not, in recent years, entertained either idea in any practical fashion.

What struck him now was the extraordinary notion of an unpredicted thing; a break in the routine of naps and cups of tea, snatches of music, regulated hours of dullness at his typewriter. It was a gift. 'Yes,' he said to Nellie Fraser, 'I would.'

She smiled. It seemed to him the first time she had looked youthful and happy and he grinned back at her. She laughed. 'That's settled then. I won't have to stay in that shitty hotel.'

Instantly he felt depressed. There was the whole day to use up. He ought not to have been so reckless. 'I shall have to work for several hours,' he said cunningly. 'That's all right, Jasper,' she said. His eyebrows curled up in alarm. She had used his first name. He thought it an appalling lack of form. 'I would ask you to dinner, but there are only frozen vegetables,' he said. 'I have become a vegetarian.' She was such a big meaty girl that he thought this must strike a substantial blow.

Instead she seemed enormously pleased and had begun writing in her notebook. 'Now that's really something,' she said. 'I guess you've given up meat for humanitarian reasons.'

'No,' he said, 'no.' But she was busy writing down what she had said and she did not hear him.

He had, in fact, given up meat because of meanness. He was horrified by the price of it in the shops. He remembered when steak was two shillings a pound. When he went out to dinner with friends, who were paying, he always had a nice fillet of steak or a sole.

She asked him about his work. 'Oh,' he moaned. It was the thing he dreaded. He had read once that women in childbirth had bouts of unconsciousness between pains and that when it was over they slept and awoke happy and he thought it was like being a writer; the boredom, the doubt, the waste of vigour that were forgotten once the book was published; the playfulness with which one began to hash about with a fresh plot.

He was being sent back to retrieve it all. It bore in on him like the aches of old age; the meanness of heart and the poorness of pocket; the clamouring of too many characters across one's clear path of vision; insignificant twerps like Harry Turtle, dancing in one's light, swelling the brain with dull rage so that in desperation one flung aside the clogged imagination and turned to real life.

It became, after all, the dry and childish art of the collector, meticulously pinning down human beings, causing them no damage but preserving forever the damage they had done to themselves, so that one's whole life, and all the people in it, was pressed out, bloodless on the page, and all the love was betrayed.

'I do very little work nowadays,' he said. 'I can't remember. It was a hard slog. There is no such thing as inspiration, except as a pleasurable form of self-abuse, reputed to lead to insanity and blindness.' He was tickled that she wrote this down. It was from one of his books. He began a game then, answering all her questions with passages from his novels. Although his memory was defective in regard to dates and people's names, he could read his novels from his head with ease. She wrote everything down. She had difficulty keeping up with him. It gave him a wicked sense of glee. He continued until the veins in her wrist bulged and then he smiled a kindly old man's smile and said: 'I must leave you now, my dear. Time for my day's quota of words.'

'Of course,' she said, exhausted.

He crept into his study and sat rigidly at his desk. He took a flask from a drawer and drank deeply of its alcoholic content. Then, when ten minutes had passed and he was certain that she was not going to burst in on him to administer his treat, he sank down on to the day bed under a woolly rug and fell fast asleep.

He woke to the sound of music and a smell of woodsmoke and spices. She had lit the fire and switched on the radio. She had done some sort of Mexican thing with his frozen food. He was disappointed because he liked the look of the separate mounds of yellow and green, corn and carrots and sprouts and beans. He brought wine to where she was sitting cross-legged on the floor by the fire. She gleamed healthily in the firelight. He sat in a chair and munched the horrible food while she talked about herself. She seemed to have finished with the interview, which was a relief. She brought him the treasures of her little life. It was like examining a collection of sea-shells. She was very fresh and boring. She drank a lot of wine and stretched like a cat. His eyes narrowed to the eye of the hunter. He reconnoitred his physical points and was relieved that his hair, though fluffy, covered his head and that the folds of his face were not gaunt or peevish. When it was time for bed he stood up and patted her on the head. She smiled, staring into the flaky fire. He told her where she could find his bedroom and then, watching the clean curve of her brow, her peaceful eyebrows, he said: 'There are three other bedrooms. Feel free . . .'

He brought a bottle of good wine to his room and two fresh glasses. He put a silk coverlet on the bed, and arranged genial lighting from some little lamps. He patted his chops with some scent stuff from a bottle. He caught sight of his weary face in a mirror and it made him laugh: 'Ha! Old blighter!' All the same he removed his warm pyjamas from under the pillow and hid them and clambered, instead, into a chilly pair of silk pyjamas which had never been used. He got into bed and lay with his hands clasped behind his head in the pose of a thinker. In a moment or two, this arrangement seized his limbs so he curled himself up into a brioche and his eyelids clamped down like bottle caps.

'Hi! I was doing the dishes.' The room exploded into light and Levingston awoke with a snort. There was someone in his room. An anchor of sleep swept him down. Young whatsit? 'Could you possibly turn off that light?' he begged.

She came and sat on the side of the bed. She reached out her fingers and swept back his hair and then lightly dipped a finger in the cleft of his chin. She smiled at him impishly.

Young girls. Young girls. Slowly he put out a hand and, scarcely touching, traced the shadow of her breasts behind her blouse. Young girls.

'Clothes,' she said, 'are such a drag. Long live the zipless fuck.' She stood up abruptly. She pulled off her blouse and dropped it on the floor. Her skin had an impervious sheen, like a modern wipe-clean surface. She was tanned all over, even her breasts, to the colour of cornflakes. It was not how he remembered the skin of a girl. He remembered the tremendous discovery of breasts beneath a blouse, the softest most beautiful flower, magnolia pale, silken; the merest touch of a finger must bruise, a careless fingernail, crush like a rose petal. No, not for fingers – only for lips. White dome, severely pristine, blushing to the ennobled conqueror. It was how it was. Oh, God, remember, the piety of lust.

He poured out two glasses of wine and tried to remember the things he used to say. 'Oh, God,' was all he could think of. 'Oh, God.' The girl bounced into bed on top of him. She made him spill a bit of the wine. He handed her a trembling glassful and she knocked it back, giggling. 'Here's to greatness,' she said. She put her wine-filled tongue into his mouth. The thrust of it was like a pickle. Her arm went beneath the blankets. The big hand descended heartily.

He put away his wine with regret and rolled on top of her. He desired to trace with his mouth the ignorant shape of her lips, but her jaws were open like a cave. He tried to pretend that she was a woman, that their ages had been divided and shared and they enjoyed the forgiving passions of middle age but she would not stop talking and her sharp little teeth champed on his tongue. 'You're a very attractive man. I've always wanted to go to bed with you as long as I can remember. Don't worry, baby.' Her hands went to his head. They felt beneath his hair the dry skin, the veins knotted by thought and they shrank away. They clawed irritably at his back and then sank with hopeless impatience to his loins.

Her fingers commenced some very efficient routine that reminded him, with a nostalgic pang, of the bursts of energy he used to take out on his typewriter very late at night.

He was passive in her hands, tired, very tired. He was amused by the optimism of her years, her determination to turn him into something else. 'It's all right,' she murmured. 'It's okay. Relax. You're beautiful.'

Ridiculous, really, the young could never accept anything. Ridiculous. He began to laugh. Put it down to tiredness. She tickled and kneaded and pulled patiently. His laugh came out like a slow, repetitive creak.

The big, useful hands froze. 'Stop that,' she said, furious. He withdrew himself gently. He wrapped his pyjamas around him comfortably and then put out a hand to pat her poor brown shoulder. She shrugged him away. 'You don't care,' she accused.

'At my age . . .' he defended mildly.

'Don't bullshit me,' she snapped.

'My dear,' he said. 'It doesn't matter. Not at all.'

Her voice tore out: 'I only went to bed with you because I didn't want to hurt your feelings. But you don't have any feelings. At least I can say I found the real Jasper Levingston. Readers, I slept with him. I think you're a disgusting old man. You've ruined everything. I shall never be able to read your books again.'

She hurtled to the other side of the bed and sighed long and tragically. After another sigh, less tragic, she was fast asleep.

About a week after her departure (he had to remind her to take her recording machine) the telephone rang. 'It's Helen,' said the voice from the wire. 'Helen?' he inquired cautiously. 'Do come up,' he said with enthusiasm. 'Come as soon as you like.' He hung up and went to write her name in his diary. He was glad to know that he was not totally befuddled. Helen always came at this time of year. She was a woman of habit.

46

He was standing by the window, his head bobbing anxiously behind the glass as he waited for his friend. 'Aha!' he cried out with glee. A small, stout woman was beating her way down the track. Her right arm sagged with a basket of things. She came to the gate and rattled.

'I thought you weren't going to come,' he said, when he had brought her into the house and was unwrapping, one by one, the treats she had brought for him to eat.

'I always come,' she said.

'I know,' he said. 'I got confused.'

'It's our anniversary,' she said.

'I'm sorry.'

She took his hand. 'My dear,' she said. 'It doesn't matter.'

He went to hunt for her favourite record and found that it was on the turntable where he had placed it a week ago in anticipation of her call. He devoured her delicious presents while she told him about her year, dripping ash everywhere from the cigarette she kept clenched in the corner of her mouth. She bred little dogs, which he loathed. She had been committed to dogs even before they had fallen in love, thirty years earlier. She took the cigarette from her mouth for a grudging moment, to kiss him, then put it back again. 'I'm very fond of you, you know,' she said: 'though I can't bear that face you get when you're thinking, that long face.'

He said: 'We should have married. We only see each other once a year, now.'

'No,' she said firmly. 'At my age I need something to look forward to.'

How wise she was, how nice. After she had been with him for a day, he always began to be irritated but then she had to get back to her dogs again and as soon as she was gone he began to miss her, and then to look forward to her return.

He waited patiently for her to finish her cigarettes and her brandy and then led her out of her ash-scattered patch and took her to bed.

'Ah, Helen,' he said. 'Ah, Helen.' When her arms went around him he did not feel that he was holding another person in his arms, merely that he was comfortably fleshed, that his bones no longer poked out.

Her wry mouth patted his lips repeatedly with a 'tut-tutting' sound, breathing sadness, breathing cigarette smoke, breathing forgiveness for the bastard he was that he had not married her thirty years ago when she loved him so much.

She never read any of his books; just as well, since she was in several of them. She had no interest in his work. It was him she loved. He had challenged her with the smallness of his heart but she considered it quite good enough for her. Lately he found himself thinking about her more and more. When she was in his arms he thought she was the good side of himself that he had been searching for all his life and he was ambitious, for a time, to become a part of her. 'Ah, Helen.'

He made it last as long as possible, barely moving, hoarding the comfort, until he cried out with relief, not that he could still be aroused but that he could still be loved.

'Ha!' Helen said. 'You're a lively old devil.'

He had her held against his chest like a hot water bottle. 'I was thinking,' he said, 'about a thing we used to have when we were boys. It was a bun made of rubber. It looked like a nice bun but when you tried to eat it, it was made of rubber. It was a trick.'

'I thought men were supposed to think of cricket,' she said sleepily. 'That's a bad sign, returning to childhood.'

It wasn't his childhood. It was the girl. He had a sudden picture of her breasts, like big brown buns, as healthy and plain as knees; the determination in her hands, pulling and rubbing like a woman doing her washing on a rock. The approach was so lacking in stealth and sequence that he forgot what he was meant to do.

What did one do with a child who was old beyond illusion?

Laugh to make her angry? Prance like Harry Turtle in the cold light of her truth.

He could not let her know that she stirred him a little less than she desired him. He could not hurt her feelings.

Appearances

The widow gave my mother a pair of boots. They were biscuit-coloured with little pointy toes darkened with polish. The heels were shaped like an apple core and gave the feet a rising curve that made me think of the neck of a pony. 'They're kid boots,' my mother said, shocked. The widow nodded. She had clutched them to her breast like infants. She handed them across. They were set in the centre of the table and the two women watched them with sadness. 'You're too good,' my mother said, confused. 'They're too good.' 'Just so they get some use,' the widow said. Her eyes found me under the table and she gave me a long look like Christ crucified, so forgiving that I had to suck my lips in over my teeth. She stood up painfully and skushed away in her black sandals.

'She was very beautiful,' my mother said. The boots still held the centre of the table, a monument to her beauty. We had arranged the tea things around them. 'Like a young Indian girl, ebony hair braided in plaits, skin the colour of honey.'

She met her husband at the post-box. They were posting letters to other people who were forgotten in that instant. Ten years later when she was thirty, he stepped in front of a motor car and turned her into a widow. She buried her beauty with him. She took a lodger in the upstairs room and sold paraffin from a shed at the end of the garden leading to the lane.

A frond of rhubarb jam dangled through a hole in my toast. I sucked it through from underneath. I had heard the story before. Each time the widow brought us an instalment of her past, mother repeated it as though it was her task to tend the memories. All I had to do was listen but I did so with a face bulging with disbelief. The widow was not beautiful. Her skin was grey. She was stooped and seamed with sadness. All women were sad but some had the toughened crusts of good old times built into them. It gave them a sense of privilege. The widow's sadness was a mildew that overgrew and enclosed her.

Her young husband took her to France on a boat. They saw the Eiffel Tower and drank wine at tables in the street. He bought her new boots, kid. Nothing was too good for her.

'Put them on. Put them on, let's see!' Mother chuckled as if she had suggested something wicked. We were both caught up in glee. I tore off my own boots with the laces still tied and flung them anywhere. The soles flapped and gaped like corner boys as they sailed across the floor. 'They're sieves! You poor daisy!' mother lamented. We doubled up with laughter.

I was eleven, nearly twelve. My legs were no longer rigid stalks of sinew. When I stretched them out one by one to pull on the boots my mother peered and frowned on their new curve and sheen. They had become miraculously fleshed and golden as a cake does in the oven. I pulled on the boots and she did the buttons. It took a long time and made us serious again. I was a big child. My feet almost filled out the dainty toes. 'Now walk,' she said. I levered myself down from the chair and took a few blunted steps – a hoofed animal. I began to giggle. Mother sighed. 'It's a shame, but they'll have to do.' I tottered over to her and stopped. 'I'll take them off now.' She did not look at me. 'No. Keep them on. You've got to get used to them.'

She started to clear the table, clattering the dishes as if I had done something to annoy her. She would not look at me. 'Your boots are in tatters,' she accused. 'You have me disgraced among the neighbours.'

Disgrace was a shameful word. To be poor was the greatest disgrace of all. My father had left us when I was four although mother always said he was working abroad. He sent us a little money now and then. Spread very thinly, it was made to do. Close to the top of our meagre shopping list came Appearances. Mother kept a tablet of Pears soap in a tin in the hot press. I could always tell when visitors were coming because I was sent to the press to bring the soap to the bathroom. I can still remember the exact feel and smell, its tortoise-shell transparency, coming out of a nest of cellophane in a butterscotch tin. Sometimes it was thin and had to be prised off with expertise like a new scab. In the end it became a golden monocle which I was allowed to take to my bath, viewing through a sepia haze the coal fire in front of which the metal tub was placed, before going to bed smelling of visitors' hands.

On the kitchen press, beside the china dog with glass eyes, the soap jar was kept. It was where mother saved up coins for a fresh tablet, knowing it was one of the few things that mattered; knowing, like everyone else, that poor people used cake soap.

She was strong and good. She was also stubborn. There were times, as now, when nothing one might say would make sense. Children had appearances to keep up, too. It was not the sort of thing one could explain to an adult. Insignificance was our aspiration. Conformity was all, the trappings of womanhood taboo. High heels were pantomime farce. They belonged to another world that did not incorporate walking, skipping, running, scuffing, climbing. Those delicate leather points had nothing to do with my own square and practical feet. It was hopeless to imagine that I could prance into school like a centaur and not be made to suffer. I would not wear them, never. I would bring my own boots in a bag and change in the park, hide the kid boots in a bush. I caught my mother's patient glance. She was sitting at the table again, very still, hands folded like flower petals. Her hands were not like flower petals but the evening sun was suddenly a flurry of pink tissue paper which lit up the frizzy gold of her hair and her pale, unhappy mouth, rose-tipped her fingers.

She smiled on my scowling rage with such pure affection and amusement that for a moment she looked lovely and I worshipped her. For a moment. I smiled, regretted it, became confused and clumped out of the room and off to bed like a pig on a pogo stick.

School was two miles from where I lived and I was given twopence each day for the tram. In the morning I walked to school and saved a penny for an Eccles cake for The Owl. Walking was no hardship. Most of the girls walked. We did not stride out with unhappy stoicism as people do today, snorting up the air as if it was a ball of string to be sucked up the nostrils in a single, tortuous breath for the good of their health. We stalked and ambled like cats, sniffing at the air without particularly taking it in, scenting incident on the wind. Girls collected girls as they streeled along. There was no organized pattern but it was not aimless. Navy blue arms intertwined. Heads bowed, profiles blurred. The girls stamped along.

'Got anything to eat?'

'Me lunch. Lay off.'

'Cheese?'

'Jam.'

'Keep them.'

'Spell "miscellaneous".'

'M-i-s-s . . .'

'That's the easy one. Gilhawley'll kill you.'

'She can't kill me.'

'No.'

'She can't kill me. She can't kill me. She can't kill me.'

'What have you got on your cheeks?'

'Nothing. What's the stuff on your eyes?'

'Nothing.'

'Are they there yet?'

'I don't know. I won't look.'

'Neither will I.'

'They're there.'

'Fools.'

'Ignoramuses.'

Two unhappy schoolboys now trotted behind. On no account would they be permitted to walk beside us for we had heard that one could become pregnant that way. We spoke to them only in insults. They did not speak to us at all. Each group of girls had a similar colony of misery bringing up the rear. They were our boyfriends.

In spite of frequent threats to our lives from the homicidal Miss Gilhawley and other unpredictable adults, I can scarcely ever remember waking with anything other than happy anticipation. There were exceptions. The morning I opened my eyes to the hateful little glittering toes of the boots was one. It took me twenty minutes to do the buttons. My fingers shook with ire. I limped downstairs and understood that there was no hope of walking to school. I would have to face The Owl without an offering.

On the tram I felt deformed with misery. The Owl had not spoken to me, had not pulled my hair. When I boarded the bus he had given my legs a shocked look, glanced at my face in angry query, but I would not look at him. I slid into a seat and stared out the window. Several times I could feel his gaze on my stupid boots and on my face as if he felt I owed him an explanation. There was nothing to say. I could not let my mother down by making him understand that we were poor. He would have to believe that I had grown mad and indifferent.

When I stepped from the platform in geriatric fashion at my stop he was still watching me that way. I wanted to race away and hide my shame. I could only mince like a Chinese lady, feeling the critical tawny eyes on my back as the tram clanged off down the street. There was a dead cat flung inside the school gates and I kicked its jammy-looking corpse with one polished toe from Paris.

The Owl was my name for our tram conductor. He was a little dark man in early middle age with strange orangey eyes and a long nose and a small, cheery mouth. In spite of liberal oiling, his black hair sprang into hundreds of small curls that resembled clusters of blackcurrants. His real name was Herbert. He did not know my name. He called me his pigeon, his herring, his little hen. The names caused a queer nervous chill in the pit of my stomach, a contradictory boiling flush on my face. I wanted to be crushed in his arms – and more – a nameless something, not imagined, deeply known. He was my Owl. Oh, how I loved him. My mind raced about miserably while my eye slumped on a page of a history book which impersonally mated myth and fact and celebrated the deaths of millions.

'Napoleonic Wars! You, Miss! You with the boots! Dates?' I had a white shirt, a wine tie and a navy gymslip. I had navy stockings and navy knickers, but boots were what Miss Gilhawley specified.

Boots were what identified me from thirty-four other girls in the class. My feet hurt, my heart hurt. I lifted hurt eyes to the teacher but she saw only the non-absorbent eyes of an idler. 'Vain and idle woman,' she hissed. 'You are the bane of my life.' I hid in the toilets during lunch, ate my brawn and biscuits in the smelly dark. When school ended I fled as fast as my crippled heels allowed, praying that I might be on the tram and on my unhappy journey home before the girls came. At the gate I tripped on the cat's corpse and landed with that peculiar flying sprawl so familiar in childhood. Blood and gravel flourished on my knees and palms. A clump of girls circled over my scattered body. They were not my friends but an opposing group, big and evil. 'She's wearing women's boots! She's wearing women's boots. Find her a husband! Put them to bed! Give her a baby!' they chanted. My two best friends hung back. They were embarrassed by my appearance and afraid of the tough girls. I glared up at their big, unkind faces, their lumpy bosoms under gymslips, their ugly knees. My hands scrabbled for some object of retaliation – and clutched. I got on my feet. I swung out in a wide arc with the dead cat, holding on to its tail, exhilarated at my perfect aim as the little, fanged, matted jaw clouted each girl's face into expressions of dumb horror.

'They're *not* women's boots,' I panted. 'They're *kid* boots!'

The pleasure of victory prepared me to withstand The Owl's indifference on the tram. He had looked at me with some curiosity when I clambered on board, muddy and bloodied in my high heels. He had glanced expectantly at my right hand to see if it guarded the baker's bag which carried his customary afternoon treat. There was no bag, no Eccles cake. He turned away and went down the aisle jingling change in his fist. I limped to a seat and concentrated on cleaning the worst of the gore from my skin with a hankie.

'Here, let me help.' A low voice close to my ear. The tram was almost empty and The Owl had settled himself on the edge of the seat opposite. He licked a rather crumpled handkerchief and began to dab at my knees. He did it with tenderness. I could only stare. His face looked different. Normally his eyes crinkled at the corners. They were wide open now, peering over my dirty knees and troublesome boots as though he had mislaid something and expected to find it concealed amidst the blood and endless buttons. 'I do like your boots,' he said softly. 'Very dainty they are.' He put his handkerchief in his pocket and scrubbed his hands together, workmanlike. 'Bloody kids,' he grumbled. 'They grow up that fast.'

When some people got on the tram he stood up very straight and moved away so briskly that I was left to wonder if I had imagined his look. He had liked my boots, though, very dainty. No one had ever called me dainty. My elongated toes pointed the way to a breathtaking world of enchantments and vanities. If I could have danced I would have danced.

Later, when I was swinging on the platform as we drew near to my stop The Owl materialized once more. 'What age are you?' he breathed against my hair. 'Thirteen.' 'Good child,' he said. 'Quite the young lady, very lovely.' He asked me if I ever took the air in the park. 'I go every Saturday,' I said rapidly. Having already lied about my age, I saw no advantage in confessing that I passed most Saturday afternoons in the cinema, spending the money I earned in the morning, lighting fires and stoves for the Jews. The boys sat in a row behind us and passed sweets to us over our shoulders.

'I could meet you there, at the pond,' he murmured. 'There's something I want to show you.' I nodded. The hammering of my heart made me feel sick. 'Good child,' he said. The pavement was still moving towards me when I jumped. I had to do a little skitter like a music-hall turn to keep my balance.

Mother noticed my cut hands and knees. She made a rueful little mouth of sympathy. 'Had a good day?' she said. I nodded. I still could not speak. She looked as if she might say more but instead she came to me and pressed my head against her breast, stroking my hair fiercely. 'Good child,' she said.

I was going to have a baby. The thought made me feel important. I would have to take the belt off my school tunic and bring a pint of milk to the classroom for my lunch. If the girls pasted me I would have a miscarriage. There would be buckets of blood on the school steps. I sat in the poky grass at the edge of the pond and scraped sugar grains from the top of an Eccles cake with my teeth. In a bag tucked into the lap of my yellow frock was another cake. That was for The Owl. The cakes had been paid for by the Jews. I got twopence for lighting their fire and putting a match to the jets on the gas cooker. Mrs Wolfson and her two daughters, Gilda and Tilly, had forsworn housework on Saturdays. The girls locked their plump fingers under their breasts and sang duets, easing their brown eyes and dimpled faces into mists of love while they smiled at their father, who was very small.

Mrs Wolfson accompanied on the piano. She kept a glass of wine on top of the instrument for her refreshment. She wore a long silk dress the colour of wine and a garland of black feathers round her neck. Her dress was cut low at the front to show breasts which rose evenly like successful loaves. The drawing-room was a treasure trove. Each piece of furniture was veiled with lace like a bride. There were glass lamps and silk cushions and little crystal dishes of sweets. After my work I was allowed to choose a sweet from one of the dishes. I had to sit in a marshy velvet sofa to eat it. Gilda sank down beside me, embracing me in ladylike smells. 'Now, who is the lucky fellow?' she said straightaway. I grimaced coyly and squirmed with rage. 'There is no fellow,' I said. 'So!' she clasped her hands and surveyed me efficiently: 'You have waved your hair for no fellow. You have put pink on your cheeks and grease on your lips for no fellow. You have borrowed someone's high-heeled boots for no fellow.' The other members of the family watched me with smiling interest. 'He is not a fellow,' I said coldly. 'He's a grown man. He wants to show me something.' The women glanced at one another darkly. Their chins drew back and their breasts billowed forward until they looked like some very peculiar birds.

'How would your mother feel if you told her some grown-up man wanted to show you his something?' Mrs Wolfson said angrily. 'I bet he's got a wife,' said Gilda. 'I bet his wife has seen enough of his something.' 'You stay away from this man,' Tilly said. 'As sure as black is white you will have a baby.'

He had a wife. I had seen them one Sunday afternoon on

the beach at Killiney with about half a dozen little currant-haired children who screamed with ragged delight at the waves. The children all had dirty faces. Even when they ran into the water and the waves broke over their heads they emerged with streaks of dirt glistening under the wet. Mrs Owl was fat. She wore a pink bathing cap and swimming costume although she stayed on the shingle. She lay back on a rug chewing sandwiches and cuddling a dirty baby. He chased the children into the water and ran back to his wife, proclaiming his pleasure with a grin. For a reply she threw back her head and chortled. I watched his squat brown figure like a modern cartoon of a peanut man, shepherding his family with mirth. His hair bubbled and gleamed like boiling oil. His amber eyes crinkled. My stomach cringed.

In the park the afternoon heat summoned up its swarm around the pond. Young women pumped the handles of prams to maintain the trussed human contents below explosion point. Courting couples crouched tensely entwined. Elderly gentlemen stepped out briskly with walking sticks and followed feebly with inefficient feet. Two boys of nine or ten blundered by in sullen grey jackets and dusty boots. Their appearance caused such a sensation of outrage among the calm possessors of the pond that they galloped off like spiders into the dank trees. If the adults saw me at all they saw a nice quiet child in a yellow dress. If I saw them, I saw them as aspects of my scenery, of no more individual significance than cows or ducks. Grown-ups were parents and teachers and people behind shop counters. I did not think of them as a part of my future any more than I thought of death. To me it was a children's world. Adults were people who were too old to be children. Deprived of all that they knew and that made them happy they grew mad and dangerous. They ate unpleasant food and emanated pungent smells. They were angry and violent and constantly had to be forgiven. Men and women locked themselves behind doors together and moaned and argued with restrained madness. They did curious things together of which children were warned but not told. The Owl was a grown man. This fact had impressed the Wolfsons greatly. Tilly had declared that I would have a baby.

In my mind's eye I could see her glistening carmine lips compressed in envy, her breasts swollen like a bolster in awe; now, in my real eye, my Owl approaching, striding past the ornamental pagoda and the flower borders, coming to show me something adult and undoubtedly curious. I felt important and curiously grown-up.

I finished a last moist and delicious mouthful of fruit and flaky pastry and licked crumbs and sugar from my lips. I brushed the skirt of my frock and spread it over my legs like a fan. A few people looked when I waved with both arms to The Owl. My Owl. He looked wonderful. He was specially dressed up in a pale cotton jacket and a blue shirt open at the throat. He plodded towards me with his head down as if it was an uphill climb. I jumped to my feet and extended my hands to him. He scowled into the grass and hurried past, in the direction of the trees where the boys had vanished. I swung my unwanted arms and stared after him, mouth gaping with hurt. After a few moments I swooped to pick up my paper bag and raced after him.

He was guarded by a circle of elms. He had taken off his jacket and it swung stylishly from a branch. He smiled at me now, his crinkly smile.

'That's right, chicken,' he said when I approached.

'You ran away,' I whined.

'Not from you, pigeon. There. I've got something to show you, something special. It is a secret. We don't want the world and his wife looking on.'

'I've brought you a cake.'

'That's my girl.'

I came to him holding out the bag in both my hands. He

did not take the bag but put his hands around my wrists and very slowly brought his mouth down to my forehead. It landed like a scrap of paper. He led me away, still holding my wrists in his hands. We wandered through dim, luminous, wooded paths. We came to a rather unpleasant part of the park where there was a dried river bed and a writhing tangle of tomato weeds. Ill-tempered walls of briar guarded the pit which had once been a piece of river. It was a place famed for unpleasantness. Children were warned not to go there. He picked me up in his arms. My long legs spilled over his limbs. He surged recklessly through the thorns, clutching my skirt in a bunch to keep it from tearing. He put me down on a mossy patch that was olive green and velvety. He sat opposite to me. Our feet touched on the ground.

'You've always been special to me,' he said.

'I love you,' I said.

'Oh, well,' he said.

'I'd do anything in the world for you. I'd die for you.'

'Hush now. Let me talk.' He reached out a hand to touch my face, but did not. His fingers traced my body without touching it. He dropped his hand to my leg and clutched the oddly curved ankle of my boot. 'You've always been different from the other kids – noisy little buggers. I feel you understand me. There's not many people understand. I'd have spoken before but I thought of you as just a little girl. Forgive me, miss ... it wasn't until you ventured into ladies' boots that I saw you as a lovely young woman. I'm a married man, of course, and you're still only a young lass but every dog's entitled to his day.'

I had begun to be afraid. I was not used to being treated as an equal with adults. It was certain to mean trouble. My mouth was dry. My limbs went prickly. I looked up at the high walls of briar, the relentlessly blue sky, praying that someone would pass or rain descend.

'Do you trust me, miss?' he said. I nodded. 'What I'm

going to show you is something very sacred, something private. You must promise not to tell a living soul.' I nodded. 'Good child.'

He began to unbutton his shirt. I stared in awful curiosity. 'Don't look yet, pettie,' he urged. 'Close your eyes and don't look until I say.' I clenched my eyes. 'Look at me now! Look at me now!' his voice commanded. I opened my eyes and slammed them shut again. I had been struck blind. Where The Owl had sat nothing remained but a blaze of light. I looked again, cautiously. The Owl was still there, a frowning blur of face in the shadows. He was dressed in a cotton vest and trousers. The entire surface of his vest was pinned with silver medals. Caught in the low rays of the afternoon sun they flashed and glimmered like unnatural fire. I clapped my hands in delight and gazed in wonder on my beautiful Owl, my wizard.

He moved closer. He caught my hand and pressed it to his metallic chest. It made a musical jangle. He said: 'You can touch them if you like.'

I began to explore the dazzling engraved miniatures. The Owl's chest was populated by a lot of unhappy-looking men and women in long dresses. Rays of light came out around them and there were messages written in Latin. 'That one's been blessed by the Holy Father in Rome,' The Owl narrated. 'This is a miraculous medal of the Blessed Virgin. Wear it at all times and it keeps you safe from harm. See the little glass door on this. It's a sacred relic of a saint. It carries a plenary indulgence to save you from hell in case of mortal sin. This is Saint Christopher, patron saint of travellers. That heart is the Sacred Heart of Jesus, burning with love for you and me. Here's Saint Jude, patron saint of hopeless cases.' Together we explored each member of his powerful and passionate family and thrilled at their magical powers. I thought I had never seen anything so wonderful in my life. The Owl said he had been a sodality man all his life. He had other medals and relics at home, hundreds. He could accommodate no more under his clothes. He had to keep them under his clothes because there were those who would snigger at holy things. His wife even smiled a bit sometimes. I was different. He had known from the start that I would understand.

I understood. I burned with understanding. I felt that The Owl and I stood alone in all the world, enclosed in a radiant shape like the Sacred Heart.

There were things I still did not understand, and after we had sat in silent understanding for some minutes I began to wonder about them. Had I now been taken across the threshold of womanhood? 'Are you giving me a baby?' I asked. I put my hands around his bristly neck and kissed him quickly to show that I did not mind. His orange eyes lit on me in astonishment. He seized my hands and pulled them roughly away. 'Bloody kids,' he complained. 'You haven't been listening to a blessed word I've said.' He tore the paper bag which was lying at my side. He took out his cake and began to chew on it, angrily and rather hungrily.

Some Retired Ladies on a Tour

'There's a man,' Alice said. 'She's with a man.' She scrubbed the bus window with a bunched-up brown stretch glove. May sat down heavily beside her, still probing a blasted peppermint. She leaned forward, her menthol breath ruining all Alice's work on the glass.

They could make him out through the window mist, a tall, pale figure, his garments worried by wind and rain. Mrs Nash was holding his hand. The thing that bothered them speechless was an aspect of his stance that was a confirmation of youth. They couldn't see him properly but he was definitely young. 'She's a nutting,' May said. 'She's nutting but thrash.'

It wasn't the first time they had talked about Mrs Nash. She turned up at the slide-illustrated lecture and told them all she had a stall at Birkenhead Market. It was a tour for retired ladies. She was the only one of them who hadn't retired although she was of an age for it. 'Mention my name and you'll get a cut,' she told them, to get pally.

Doris Moore had a laugh about that. Up to the summer she had been manageress at Imperial Meats. 'Mention my name and you'll get a cut,' she said with a wink that pleated her turquoise eyeshadow like a quilt.

Forty years she had been with Imperial. When she left they gave her a set of cut sherry glasses. She put them out on the kitchen table at home and filled them each to the brim with whisky. Not a drop was spilled when she drank them. She was quite proud of that. Out of the blue she had a vision of her first day at Imperial. She was fourteen when she stepped through the metal doors and began a novice's jiggle against the chill. They were all looking at her bow-tied blouse that was the colour of red currants. The men wore aprons covered with blood. The women, their noses blue under powder, wore mountains of jumpers and folded their arms over their wombs to protect any life that might be there. Not that many of them married. There was a habit that came with working in the cold, of not changing underwear every day.

By the time she was thirty, Doris realized that she hadn't bothered to look for a man. She had been too busy looking for jumpers. Her big achievement was learning to knit. She came to look on the cold as a constant; warmth and sunshine were interruptions. At the slide-illustrated lecture, she was the one who asked if the hotels had central heating. 'That's all right, then,' she said, when the man apologized for the fact that they had not.

She was the youngest of the ladies but retired all the same. At fifty she woke moaning with rheumatism. She developed a cough that wouldn't go away. At fifty-four she got pleurisy and the doctor ordered her to leave Imperial. After he had tapped on her chest she put back on her jumpers and sat in front of him crying. She couldn't go and work in an office or a shop, not with the central heating. He helped her to get a disability pension. She managed with that and the home knitting, which wasn't taxed. It was quite nice, really. She began to do up her face and to wear fancy knits.

Alice and May had latched up with Doris from the start. They all took a drink and could enjoy a laugh. Doris was something of a star. She had discovered quite late a talent for making people laugh out loud. It was her appearance of not giving a damn. Few people realized that deep down she really didn't give a damn.

She sat in a seat in front of Alice and May. She had actually seen Mrs Nash and her man before the others but she didn't let on. She didn't want to watch Alice's glove fretting him into sharp relief. She preferred looking at him through the condensation on the window, thinking his beige outline like a young Alan Ladd; thinking the way he held on to Mrs Nash was more like a blind person than a beau; thinking that of all of them he was most of an age with her. She watched until they started to move towards the bus and then she tossed her head back so that the tassle on her purple knitted hat boxed May playfully on the cheek. 'Mention her name and you'll get a cut,' she said loud enough for the whole bus to hear because she knew that everyone had been looking. When Mrs Nash stepped on to the bus the retired ladies were all laughing. She laughed delightedly with them and then trailed off, uncertain, because they stopped laughing quite abruptly.

They were looking at the man. Unless your taste was in your mouth you'd have to admit he was handsome, Doris said later. He was about forty-five with light curly hair and a boyish, diffident smile. The ones who were most aware of him glared huffily and looked away. The motherly ones smiled to make him at ease. Mrs Nash could see they were admiring him. She grinned proudly under her green Crimplene turban. 'She has a nice smile,' Alice said, easily wooed by a show of good cheer. May clicked on her mint reprovingly. Mrs Nash held up the man's hand as if he was a winner in a boxing match or else an item for auction. 'This is Joe,' she said. 'He's my son.'

The drive was a disappointment. They had expected the driver to be a comedian who would take them all on, call them darling, sing over the microphone so they could join in and jolly up the shy ones. Instead there was a snivelling young pup who got his thrills speeding around corners and wouldn't stop to let them go to the toilet. By the time they got to the first resort the outgoing ones were bored and bad-tempered. The eldest ladies were purple and rigid with misery.

He pushed them out of the bus and disappeared into a pub. They found themselves teetering on the edge of a cliff and stood there shivering, staring down at the sand that curved in a thin ribbon around the base, yellow in the twilight, like custard poured on a pudding. 'Bloody hell, where's our hotel?' carped May. 'Across the road, you daft old toad,' Doris guffawed, her sharp eyes picking out the 'Cliff Palace' as specified in the brochure, although the description they had been given did not tally with the outward appearance of the hotel, which looked fat and pink and putrefied.

The younger ones marched across the road with loud complaints and laughter, purposefully heading for the bar. The older ones shuffled and scuttled and snuffled and grumbled. Mrs Nash looked hopefully at the first batch and guiltily at the second. She and Joe walked to the hotel alone, holding on to each other.

At reception there was a bit of commotion that made them forget all about the dismal journey. Mrs Nash was having a row with the receptionist. There'd been a mistake, she said. Her son had been put in a separate bedroom.

The blotched young woman behind the desk pressed her fingers on the edge of the wood in desperation and clung on with her thumbs. A man in a suit came down the stairs and the girl gave him an imploring look. 'She wants to sleep with her son,' she blurted, making it sound much worse than the young couples that came in the season. The manager looked at the agitated sea of post-sexual female flesh, at the shrivelled face under the potty green hat. Christ. He couldn't have cared less if she wanted to sleep with a Marmoset monkey. He wondered about the bloke, though.

He sidled warily past the grannies and crouched beside the girl at reception, his closeness making fresh blotches on her complexion. 'They can have thirty-seven,' he said, with a glance at the book. He took a key from a hook on the wall and held it out to Mrs Nash on his little finger. She took it with a grateful smile but Doris Moore had noticed his sneer. 'Any notion of rooms for us or are you going to make us sleep on our feet like blasted horses?' she said, loudly and rudely, causing a titter among the ladies. Doris had the knack all right. 'Not until you've had your oats, dear,' said the manager, quick as you like, and those who understood shrieked with delight.

Dinner was very nice. There was a lovely mushroom soup followed by roast turkey and a choice of trifle or bread and butter pudding with cheese as an extra. Alice was finished first and she took her cup of tea into the residents' lounge because she wanted a seat by the fire. As she left she had the impression of something dark scuttling behind her like a spider. She turned to find herself gazing at the green turban. 'A drink! You've got to have a drink,' Mrs Nash said, grinning triumphantly as if it was a forfeit. Joe, behind her, seemed a transparent creature, a daddy-long-legs, but her cordiality was echoed in his smile. Alice knew what May would think but her mouth was watering for a gin and orange. 'All right, then, while I'm waiting for my friend,' she said.

'Friends are very nice,' Mrs Nash said, when she was settled into the fire, sucking her port. 'I haven't got many friends. Account of Joe.' 'Oh, yes?' Alice said with a kindly look at Joe who seemed miles distant from them, smiling at the flames and taking sips at his glass of lager. Alice was having a very nice time. The drink was a large and she was going to be the one who would tell the others about Mrs Nash and her man.

On his way to work, Joe had fallen down with a clot, Mrs Nash told Alice. He was brought home in a bread van and she remembered noting a stack of coconut cream sponges and having a silly urge to buy one for when he came to. A clot, the doctor said, which was working its way to his brain. You couldn't tell when it would strike. Next time he'd be a goner. She ought not to let him out of her sight.

She had watched him asleep on the sofa. His feet were up on the olive green Dralon that she was paying off at nine pounds a month. It was the sofa that reminded her Joe was the only thing that had ever actually belonged to her. She wasn't about to let him go to a clot. The clot wouldn't dare strike while she was around.

Alice fished a slice of orange out of her empty glass and severed the flesh from the rind slickly with her false teeth. She was planning how she would tell May that you could never judge on the face of things. She didn't have long to wait. As she tipped the glass on her tongue to catch the tantalizing residual taste of alcoholic boiled sweeties, May stormed in, making demolition noises as she crunched on her peppermints in a rage.

'I hope I'm not interrupting something,' she said savagely. Alice didn't know where to put herself. 'I told Mrs Nash I was waiting for you,' she entreated. 'She's been telling me about her son.' She could only hope the implications would sink in and have a soothing effect. May was too hopping mad to hear. There was malice in the way she munched on her mints. Mrs Nash pawed gently at the sleeve of the fawn woollen cardigan that covered her son. 'Is it time you went to the lav?' she said. Joe returned from his dreams without any perceptible change to his expression. He drained his lager and stood up, holding hands with his mother. 'We're going to the toilet,' he smiled at the ladies.

Doris, who had just come into the lounge with the stragglers, couldn't restrain herself. 'Enjoy yourselves,' she called out. When the two of them were gone Doris went into a fit of indrawn croaks that in a girl would have passed for giggles. 'He winked at me,' she squawked, when the fit had subsided. Alice couldn't tell if he had or not but she was cross with Doris for taking the good out of what she had to say and May's sulk was making her edgy.

'Don't be silly,' she snapped. 'That was just a reflex – like a chicken running about when its head's been cut off.'

Doris was off again, creaking like a wheelbarrow left out

in the rain. 'That's right,' she said. 'Cut off his head. Cut off everything while you're at it. Mention her name and you'll get a . . .' And the residents' lounge was filled with exhausted titters.

There was no getting any good out of her when she was in that sort of a mood. Alice went and switched on the television and sat in silence through half of a film about Vikings. Most of the ladies had gone to bed by ten. A few of them fell asleep in soft armchairs, which was a problem for management to deal with. Mrs Nash and Joe did not return at all. When Alice and May had the fire to themselves Alice lashed out on two gins and settled down to trade her latest piece of intelligence for a return to her friend's favour. 'I've got news for you,' she said. 'Concerning what?' May said, moodily. 'Concerning Mrs Nash and her son,' Alice wheedled.

May drained her glass in a gulp, screwing up her face against the sting. She snatched her white PVC handbag, which seemed to be writhing in some private torment on the arm of her chair as the firelight explored its folds. 'Listen to nutting she says,' she hissed, before marching off, leaving Alice alone with the task of forgiving everybody.

For those who could remember or to whom it concerned, the beginning of the holiday was like the first days at boarding school. Things got better with each day that passed. The ladies formed into gaggling groups and saved places at table for their special friends. The bad bits turned into laughing matters. They made jokes about the brat of a bus driver and the three days spent in a boarding house in Cornwall that was run by a widower. At breakfast they came down to plates of cold prunes and custard. After dinging the pristine plastic façade of chilly vanilla sauce with their spoons one or two of the ladies chewed on the fruit, which had not been properly soaked, before sliding a ragged brown mess out under cover of a paper napkin and immersing it as best they could beneath the custard. Next morning the prunes and custard were back again. They could tell it was yesterday's breakfast because of the breaks in the custard.

When the same brown and yellow preparation came up as a proper pudding on day five in a different location, Doris Moore whispered across the tables, 'He sent them on,' and the dining room shivered with mirth. The waitress, who had legs the colour and shape of sausages of salami, couldn't for the life of her see that prunes and custard were a laughing matter.

In the evenings there were concerts. Alice, who used to do a turn in amateur dramatics, recited a monologue entitled *If I was a lady, but then I'm not*. Most of the ladies sang a song, which was a sort of exquisite agony. They knotted their fingers in their laps and became marble-eyed with nostalgia. Their voices sailed up at the light bulb, as fragile and dreary as moths. A Mrs Dunbarr accompanied on the piano. That was the nice thing about seaside hotels, always a piano. For her role as concert pianist, Mrs Dunbarr brought out a black moiré gown with batwing sleeves that flowed and billowed over her brittle mauve fingers as they plundered the keys for Old Favourites.

Mrs Nash had a repertoire of love songs which she sang to her son, gazing into his face as if he was Nelson blooming Eddy. The real surprise was Joe. You couldn't get him to speak, never mind sing. But he responded to his mother's serenade with a song about a fellow in love with two girls, rocking back and forth, as earnest as a schoolboy. There was a line that went: 'One is my mother, God bless her, I love her.' He would pause and purse his nicely-made lips to kiss the crumpled pink sponge clumsily parcelled in green. Nothing could come up to that. The ladies clapped until their fingers pained them. Joe, strained by the excitement would crown it by announcing to all that they were going to the toilet. 'Enjoy yourselves,' the ladies chorused, made bold by

Doris Moore and their alcoholic treats, sluiced with lime or lemon or orange.

Aside from that, nobody took much notice of Mrs Nash. She didn't seem to fit. She courted Alice at a distance with gin and orange sent via the waitress. Alice was torn. You couldn't budge May, though. That blasted, savage gnashing of peppermints when her back was up was not a thing you could ignore.

By the end of the week, just when Alice was beginning to enjoy herself, she found she was also getting homesick. For two nights she had slept in a room with a curiously shaped alcove that prevented the bed from fitting flush with the wall. The bed-head was missing and her pillows fell off in the middle of the night, which woke her up. She lay alert in the dawn, heartbroken for the weight of her cats on her feet and the mingled smells of mould and ivy that were the breath of the house where she had lived from birth. She found herself worrying about Doris Moore.

You could go off Doris, she discovered. No longer tired and frightened, the ladies lacked incentive for communal mirth and Doris looked for new means of drawing attention to herself. She went on and on about Joe. He winked at her. He got her in a corner and told her she was his type. He no longer looked at his mother when he sang his song, but at her. May thought it was a joke, a laugh at the lad. Alice found it got her goat, even though she didn't say as much. She could only consider the mental betrayal of her friend as a flaw in herself and it gnawed at her in the small hours, a pain sharp as wind.

It was the second last day of the holiday. Alice was up at seven, tormented by the bed and her nagging conscience. She allowed herself a cardigan under her woolly dressing-gown and shuffled to the window in slippers to watch the sun come up. She didn't find it poetic. She was too old. Alice didn't like the violent orange globe that thrust out of the sea. The ocean ought to be the colour of an army blanket, not pink or blue like paraffin. She dressed as slowly as possible, adding a brooch to the bodice of her frock, some peculiar purplish rouge to her cheeks. Time dawdled along with her. It was only half past seven when she went down to annoy the staff for breakfast.

The first thing to hit her in the eye when she entered the dining room was the green hat. After the relief at not being first down, there came the pleasurable anticipation of forbidden fruit. She hurried to join the lone diners. 'Joe and me likes an early breakfast,' said Mrs Nash through mouthfuls of fried bread and bacon. 'We're not too gone on all them others,' she confided. 'You're all right though.' She embraced Alice with a loving glance and added affectionately: 'You're looking desperate.' Alice told her about the faulty bed and her lack of sleep, though not about Doris Moore, which was just as well because Doris sashayed through the swing doors just then, togged out to the teeth in maroon angora.

'Enjoying the worms?' she said in a preoccupied fashion, all eyes for Joe. Alice looked at her doubtfully. 'It's rashers,' Mrs Nash said, giving no quarter. She shrugged impatiently and sat down, snatching up the menu in an ill-tempered fashion. Joe glanced at her several times and began to titter. 'I get it,' he whispered. 'The early bird catches the worm.' 'You're soft,' she said in a gently mocking way that was not like her.

Mrs Nash and Alice were deep in conversation. Alice was beginning to think of her as a buddy. At her age she couldn't afford to be class conscious. When she got back home she might give May the bullet. Mrs Nash made much of her, made her feel like somebody. She wanted to give Alice her bed-head and was promising to bring it around in the night. Alice, feeling the holiday needed a climax, said she would have a noggin of gin in the room so they could have a party – a midnight feast. She felt a twinge of guilt at not having included Doris, but she needn't have worried. There was no trace of umbrage in the cracked moon face framed with fluffy wine-coloured wool. The silly thing was in a world of her own, muttering and creaking, making a perfect fool of herself with Joe Nash.

Doris hadn't got anything in particular in mind, though like Alice, she felt the holiday hadn't reached its peak. There was drinking during the day. They could afford to lash out with the holiday almost at an end. She was a bit tiddly that night when she went to bed at eleven. Undressing proved a difficult business so she hung up the maroon angora, patting it with her hand on the hanger, and left it at that. She fell asleep thinking of Joe; his nice hair, his admiring eyes, knowing full well it was the only way to have a man, where you wouldn't have to come face to face with his resentments.

At twelve she was awake again, pitched into alertness by a hellish noise that came from the end of the corridor – a scraping and rattling loud enough to wake the dead. Doris sat up, allowing the freezing air to invade the pinhole ventilations in her wool vest. The first twinge of rheumatism brought her back to earth. She swung out of bed, cursing, groped in the dark for a hairy grey dressing-gown and roped herself into it. In the middle of knotting the cord she was taken with a fit of laughing. It dawned on her; it was Mrs Nash and her blooming bed-head.

She tiptoed to the door and opened it a crack. Mrs Nash was in the corridor, dragging her burden as valiant as an ant. Doris had to stuff a hand over her mouth. She thought she would die. Over a lavishly flower-printed pair of pyjamas, Mrs Nash had on the green hat. A bloody sheikh!

When the shuffling and scraping receded, Doris let herself out into the corridor, shutting the door without a sound. If anyone should see her she was on her way to the toilet. Actually she was going to visit Joe. In fifty-four years she had not been kissed – not properly – by a man. It would make the holiday. She wouldn't tell May and Alice and them. They would say 'be your age!' When she got home she would ask round the girls from the factory, break open a bottle and give them all a laugh.

She knew the room. She tapped at the door and walked straight in. 'Joe,' she called, not able to see in the dark. She felt between two single beds for a locker and switched on the lamp that was there.

Joe was curled up in his blankets like a child, fast asleep, worlds away. She touched his hair with her fingers, a curious, damp, disturbing feel. 'Joe!' He opened his eyes and looked at her in alarm, immediately turning his gaze to the bed that had become his mother's by occupation. 'Your Mam's gone to see Alice,' she explained. 'I thought I'd come and keep you company.'

'I was asleep,' he said. 'Mother gave me a pill.' Doris was disappointed with his reaction and her bare feet were frozen solid. 'Hey, why are you latched on to her all the time?' she said. Her voice came out a bit sharp. 'Are you cold?' he asked her. 'Bloody frozen.' She dabbled her toes on the hurtful, shiny floorcover.

He threw back a portion of bed-covers, showing himself respectably covered in nice striped pyjamas. 'You better get in.' Doris gave him her hard-bitten grin. She didn't want more on her plate than she could handle but there was nothing in his approach to suggest anything underhand. She undid her dressing-gown and laid it on his mother's bed before clambering into the small, warm space beside him.

He was leaning on his elbow, not quite sitting or lying, and smiling at her. She couldn't think of a damn thing to say. His hand rested lightly on her waist, a soft, woolly hump of flesh. She was wary but as far as she could tell there was no harm in it. He took his hand from her hip and touched her lips, pressing them with a finger as if to kill an insect. He kissed her; patted her mouth with lips as warm and soft as bath towels. Doris relaxed. She sighed with relish. Romance was something, by heck it was.

They lay in silence, not speaking, just touching enough to warm one another. From the corner of her eye she saw it coming but alarm was too far from her mind to be summoned. Something reared up and launched itself at her like a dervish. 'Joe!' she cried, as if calling to him for help.

Joe had her pinned down with his bones. His tongue went into her mouth. He ran his hands over her body, under her vest and bloomers, going to places that weren't allowed. His foraging hands found her breasts, warm round cotton cannonballs.

As soon as his mouth was off hers, Doris dug her fingers into his hair and wrenched back his head. 'Here you! What the hell do you think you're at?' she hissed, not wanting to shout and wake up the whole hotel. He waited until her shuddering lessened and began arranging the peroxide curls on her forehead. 'You mustn't mind me,' he said gently. 'I'm a bad boy. That's why my Mam sticks with me.' He was smiling in that pleasing, diffident way but she was too close to him to be fooled. Even in the dim light she could see that his eyes were cold as lumps of haddock. Doris summoned up her old self and slapped on a smile. 'You're a fast operator, you are,' she said. 'I'm not that sort of girl, you know. I only came in here to get warm.' She could see his face misting over again, that suffusion of sex that made him look like the living dead. Bloody hell! The last thing to do was remind him of herself. She took a deep breath. 'Your Mam seems a good sort,' she said. 'I'd say she's a most unusual woman. You know, the way she stays with you, thick and thin.'

'The doctor said she had to,' he said pleasantly.

She rumpled his irresistible curls and began to feel capable again. 'Poor old Joe,' she cooed. 'Not well, are you?'

'Haven't you heard?' he said. 'My mother tells everyone. A clot that's working its way to my brain? I could drop down dead any minute.' His fingers reached for the sympathy of her breasts. Doris didn't care for that but she felt she had an advantage now and could handle him. 'Well you'll have to cut this class of caper for a start,' she said lightly. 'You could wreck your health.'

She attempted to remove his hands but he thrust her away and was kneading her greedily. His breathing had gone funny again and Doris could feel her heart trying to escape from beneath the monstrous hands that were squeezing private parts of her body as if they were lumps of wet washing. He began to laugh. She could feel his pleasure in her fright. 'My Mam's a liar,' he said. 'There was never a clot. There was a body.'

Doris tried to think about her maroon dress, so sad on its hanger, like a little woolly beast put outside the door for the night. She drove her mind into the chill closets of Imperial. Nothing could stop the chill that was growing inside her, strangling her guts, and threatening to stop her heart, feeding the pleasure of this strange man perched so incongruously on her stomach.

He kept rubbing himself on her. She felt he was sharpening himself to do her an injury. He was giggling. 'The judge sent me up for five years for treatment. Doctor didn't want to let me out. He didn't think it was safe. My Mam swore she'd never let me out of her sight if they let me go. And the woman was dead. There was no bringing her back.'

Doris began to scream. The scream came from deep inside her, a place that was not obedient to her mind, so that even though her brain knew it was better to die than have the whole hotel gallivanting in to find you in bed with a man, her lungs sent out foghorn signals of fright. The manager was first to arrive. Mrs Nash scuttled past him with her green hat askew in a nest of pins and hair as grey and rusty as an old Brillo. Her little black eyes darted about like insects. Splat! She clapped hands with authority. Doris's mouth slammed shut. The monster glided off her and cringed against his pillows. He looked about anxiously. The green hat was a beacon. He searched beneath it and found what he was looking for. The minuscule mouth, like a rubber band on a bunch of flowers, stretched up and up in a smile. By the light of a boarding-house bulb, Joe's returning smile, gluey with tears, was that of a four-year-old.

The whole bus was there to witness the reconciliation, the driver leering like a gorilla as Doris Moore slid out of bed and buried her shameful body in the grey dressing-gown. When Doris had brazened it as far as the door Mrs Nash turned and grinned at the retired ladies in a most menacing fashion. 'Nightie-night, now,' she said cheerily. They fled.

Early in the morning she left with Joe. They went home all the way in a taxi. They got no breakfast. The ladies knew that because those who couldn't sleep for excitement came down breathless and bleary at seven. They were shunted off back to bed like children on Christmas morning. 'Jesus save me from geriatrics,' said one frowsy scullion to another in full hearing of the ladies. 'Leaping from bed to bed in the night, down at six with their daft sons for taxis to Liverpool and banging about for breakfast at seven. Roll on the summer couples with more on their minds than breakfast!'

Doris Moore had more on her mind than breakfast. The coach had been revving a full five minutes and those with bad memories of the outward trip were wanting to go back and spend a penny when she appeared at the hotel entrance. She was wearing her purple, that she had on the first day. She was a big woman. Two heavy suitcases dangled from her hands like balloons.

She set down the cases and spent a long time smoothing her knitted gloves. The leaden day hung on her for colour. The wind whipped her blonde curls about in a flirty manner like scraps of paper in the street. Her woolly fingers retrieved her luggage and she stepped out briskly. When she boarded the bus the ladies jostled for a look, feeling nervous and foolish as if she was the queen. She pretended to be hell-bent on finding a seat. Her cherry-coloured lips drooped. Alice wanted to make a space for her. She attempted to move her heavy coat and her paper carrier bag of gifts and mementoes which were on the seat in front but May's hand shot out to restrain her. 'Don't you lift a hand for that hussy,' she threatened. 'Don't do nutting for the likes of her.'

Doris jerked her chin up and glared at May. Her eyes were glittering. Behind the sullen mask there was a look of triumph to them. She was lording it over them as a woman of experience.

She sat in the place that was saved for Alice's bag in spite of May. After hefting her own cases on to the overhead rack she shoved Alice's things to one side and shimmied her large knitted shape into the seat in an insolent fashion.

The bus was paralysed into quiet. When the vehicle whistled around corners the ladies rattled from side to side, uncomplaining. No one rustled a mag., sucked on their teeth, rendered down a peppermint. 'Well, you never can tell,' was what Doris said when their waiting was over. Everyone looked at their laps in order to ignore her properly. Doris speculated upon her knitted fingers with a rueful sneer. 'He seemed a nice enough lad, I mean.' The ladies looked out of the windows, observing Doris only through cracks in their conscience. 'People like him should be locked up for their own good. Stark, staring, raving . . .' She succeeded in luring a few watery eyes from under fragile shells. She sighed, genuinely perturbed. She could tell what they were thinking; that if such things had to happen it was better that they should happen to little silly seventeen-year-olds who really couldn't be expected to know better. She snorted. 'He killed a woman once. He could've done me in.' Doris's face burrowed into her gloves. She had unwittingly revived the demons of the night. She was fed up. It occurred to her that after all there wasn't much to tell. She wanted things to be like they were at the start, with her as the star and everyone in top form enjoying her jokes and getting in the mood for a drink when they stopped for lunch. All she had done was make them miserable and herself look a prize blooming fool into the bargain.

She started to sing. 'Show me the way to go home –' a stern hymnal beat, voice like a vacuum cleaner. 'I'm tired and I want to go to bed ...' From nowhere, another voice – a *man*'s voice. The ladies' faces twitched towards the driver in unison, eyes wide with astonishment. His virile tones surged through the bus like central heating. He took his eyes off the road to leer round at Doris. 'Come on, darling,' he encouraged, beckoning with a hand. Doris shimmied up the aisle, singing loudly, clapping her hands in time. She sat beside the driver, boldly taking the microphone from its stand and pressing the switch. 'WEEE-WON'T go home 'til morning,' she led off afresh with deafening volume, grinning coarsely into the knowing features of the youth.

Alice's feet began to move. She couldn't help it. They always got a life of their own when there was music. She hadn't realized that she was actually singing until May's white handbag rocketed into her ribs. By then it was too late. The whole busload had been infected. A frail, chalky choir of celebration, hermetically sealed into the luxury bus, pledged that it wouldn't go home 'til morning.

Home. The word died on her lips with such suddenness that it left a picture. It was her little house with its smells of mould and ivy, its two cats which received with democratic indifference her argument or endearment; and rising now like thick brown soup to soak up these familiar images and even the sounds of merriment on the bus, its silence. 'I don't want to go home,' Alice thought in a panic. 'I'm lonely.'

She tried to remind herself of the price people pay for companionship; the dreadful shame of Mrs Nash's secret,

Doris Moore's damaged reputation. 'It's a bargain!' was all she could think. But she pulled herself together very quickly and sang out. 'We won't go home 'til morning!'

And so say all of us.

Ears

'Father's ears have been at him,' Hilda said.

It was lunch time with lamb chops in the season of lamb chops. George and Hilda sat by a bay window which showed a day of bluebells and daffodils, blue and yellow like the sky and the sun. Out of doors people wore old hats and scratched at the soil for its pleasure and theirs. Compared to George's garden with its polished lawns, disciplined borders and black velvet islands of voluptuous shrubs, their gardens were mere sandpits but all he could see as he looked through the window was a sky growing black with bats.

'Beg pardon, dear?' he said.

'Me Dad,' she said. 'It's his ears.'

By and large George was a happy man. He had a strict mind; he had his garden. He had, as a sort of levy on his good fortune, Dad, the most loudly decomposing old man in history.

With a ready sigh he laid down his knife and fork and rinsed his teeth with a reasonable Beaujolais to free them from particles of meat. 'What seems to be the matter?' he articulated, baring his teeth on the 'ees' in a hope of frightening her to death.

'He says they've gone kind of soft and wet.'

In the shed, Sid Millar edged the tip of his finger under a lip of rubber in a genital shade of pink. Excitement knocked the breath out of his body in noisy jets upon which the brown and grey twigs of his moustache danced up and down. A piece of pink flipped back revealing one perfect white paw. 'Exceptional,' he wheezed. 'Exceptional.'

The second paw was simple. Working with the loose piece of rubber he folded back a second edge. Thlok! Two paws. He rolled away the rest of the rubber deftly, lovingly, like silk hose from a hooker. That was the easy bit; a fat rump with a powder-puff tail and a face he recognized with affection, returning its grotesque grin as he sighted the perfect, pointy nose and wide-set eyes.

Containing his smile in the edges of his moustache he closed his eyes and placed his fingers on the two projections that remained sheathed in rubber. He held the tips firm to avoid stress and teased the rubber upward with the fingers of his free hand. 'Phwsh, phwsh, phwsh,' went his breath and the tobacco-stained dancers rose and fell. There was a tricky bit at the end that was like taking off socks without turning them inside out. The rubber came away and Sid stood, eyes shut tight, clutching his hand to his heart for strength.

He looked. 'Oh, my God,' he said. It was a Robin among plaster rabbits. There wasn't an air hole, a distortion, a chip in sight. The ears were like sails, tall, straight, contoured. 'I've done it!' He let out a cackle, wicked in its conceit and did a dance of worship around his perfect rabbit. The rabbit looked so real you could almost see its ears twitching. They *did* twitch; first a sort of outward jerk and then a slow downward droop until they resembled boomerangs. 'Oh, my God,' Sid said. The ears curved a fraction more and dropped off on to the table. The old man touched the fractured pieces and emitted a 'phwsh' that did not move his moustache at all.

'It's no good,' he said. 'I can't do that there ear.'

'You're not to say "that there 'ere". Father doesn't like it.' The voice came from another face which rested on the table. Unlike the rabbit, this face was perfect in every detail and had lasted ten years. 'Not "ere", Edith. "Ear".' Sid pulled at his lobes for the benefit of his granddaughter. 'Rabbits don't have to have ears,' she said. 'Venus de Milo had no arms.'

'Arms,' Sid said. 'They'd be tricky right enough.' He lifted the rabbit gently from the table and laid it to rest on a shelf along with twenty or so others which ranged in quality from a small ghost foetus at the edge to some really splendid fat fellows. None of them had ears.

'Van Gogh had only one ear,' Edith's voice sailed up at him like a gnat. Sid Millar was eighty. It was a time in life when everything in his body seemed to be enjoying final bouts of independent activity which collectively brought his movements down to a totter.

His arteries were hardening, his ulcers bleeding, his toes weeping, his bones going brittle. Oh, and much more. Hilda could tell you. He was turning into a tenement. The result of watching his organs racing each other to an undignified finish gave Sid an overwhelming desire to possess, before it was all over, something of his own that was perfect. There was Hilda, of course. Sid gave a malicious snort of mirth. Hilda had no whatsits. George, damn the misbegotten Mobeydick, hadn't even got a chin.

Edith, from behind, saw her grandfather's shoulders shaking. She thought he was crying. It was a terrible thing, she had once heard, for a man to cry.

On the following morning, which was Monday, it was still spring, a fact which had not penetrated the newsroom of *The Reflection*. Tuohy and Hughes were conspiring over a copy of *The Moon*, in particular a picture of Miss Topsie Thompson, who was wearing a watch. 'What do you make of her?' Tuohy's little marble eyes rolled and his Kerry accent raked the fug of the newsroom air.

'She's a little bit skimpy,' Hughes said. His face was the colour of boiled tripe and he had a straw hat with a dog daisy in the band.

'Ja-a-aysus!' Tuohy yawned and beat his little fists on the air. 'If she was on fire I wouldn't piss on her to put her out.' Tuohy huddled over his big, black typewriter, resembling a wet cloth thrown on top of a stove, where someone had meant to wipe it and had forgotten. Everything about Tuohy, except his typewriter, was small. His malevolence, however, was magnificent. It extended not only to rival newsmen but to women and children, pet cats and stray dogs. He was the best human interest man in the business.

Little Freddie came out of the editor's office looking for tea bags and waving a memo. It was from Mr Pottle, the editor, and appeared to be a matter concerning rabbits' ears.

In his office Mr Pottle, an enormous man with a florid face and fearsome eyes was simpering at another piece of paper, pink and grubby and written upon in a pencilled print. He launched it across the desk so that it drifted into Tuohy's grey claws. 'Is it clear?' he bellowed. Tuohy read the letter through twice. Frowning so that his features became a tiny pile of dried fruit in the centre of his face, he wrestled for understanding. It was about as clear as a pint of Guinness.

'*Dear Sir,*' read the note; '*my grandfather is eighty years old and has a rubber mould of a rabbit. He tried to make one with casting plaster and found it set very quick but as the days went by it got kind of soft and wet, especially the ears which then fell off. Could you please tell him what to use as he wants rabbits to put in the garden.*'

It was signed, faithfully, by a Miss Edith Parker. Tuohy couldn't believe his ... 'Ears?'

'The plight of the elderly!' sang Mr Pottle. 'How do we lighten their twilight years, those worthy citizens who have expended their energies in the interest of making Britain great? How do we pay back the pals of our cradle days? How do we make our senior citizens smile? Who cares?'

'If the answer is "nobody" then why the hell are you going on about it?' Tuohy said nastily.

'Pensions are going up,' Mr Pottle said. 'We've got a potential readership among the over-eighties, particularly with our "no sex" policy. This is going to be gold from the oldies. The entire story will be in fourteen point for the short-sighted,' he dreamed. '*The Moon* is going to be sorry it ever bared a breast.'

Edith was swinging on the gate when she saw the two men struggling down the street; the nasty-looking little one with the notebook and the stooping, sad-faced one who was weighted down with cameras. For the purpose of the Campaign, Tuohy had been mated with Mitchell, an elderly, taciturn photographer with a modest cavity of a mouth from which nothing ever issued but a pipe. With the perception of small girls on spring days, Edith knew they were coming to her house.

George sprang through the front door at the precise moment they reached the gate, as though he had been watching from a ground-floor window which, indeed, he had. With enormous effort Tuohy extended his mouth from ear to ear in a hideous grin and extended a claw. 'Sir,' he said. 'We require your assistance in a matter of national importance. We are representatives of *The Reflection*.'

'Gentlemen?' George said in a manner calculated to assure them that they were not. Tuohy pursed his eyes in an atrocious fashion to convey human interest. 'It concerns your garden,' he said.

George had always secretly dreamed of seeing his lawn featured on the cover of *Gnomes and Gardens*. Now it had come to this. His floral displays were to be flaunted in the centre pages of *The Reflection*. He would have none of it. 'I have nothing to say,' he said sternly.

'Rabbits' ears!' Tuohy thrust. 'Do they have a place in your garden?' Lambs' Ears the fool meant, George despaired. He allowed himself a moment's yearning for that most submissive of all his shrubs, its infinitely tactile leaves yielding season after season the softness that men grew up believing to be exclusively the rewards of love. 'A pride of place,' he said, before turning on his heel and striding away indoors.

As soon as she was certain her father was out of sight,

Edith came forward. 'I know what you want,' she said. 'It's me.'

On the Wednesday following, *The Reflection* dropped the bombing of the British Library to page three and spiked the latest post-mortem developments in John Kennedy's sex life.

Instead they led on '*The Broken Rabbits that Almost Broke an Old Man's Heart!*' There was a lovely picture of Sid Millar and his granddaughter Edith standing in a typical English garden at a perfect flower border surrounded by twenty rabbits with no ears. It was a pity they couldn't have had a photograph of the son-in-law who offered the quote: 'They have pride of place in my garden!' Still, it was a smashing story and *The Reflection* with its slogan: 'The Paper that Cares about the Old' was sold out as soon as it hit the stands.

Letters poured in in their thousands. Kind people suggested alternative hobbies for Sid. Sackloads of rabbits, cloth ducks, pandas, were sent to him for comfort. Parcels of porpoises came in. To highlight the financial plight of pensioners *The Reflection* started up a 'Quid for Sid' fund. Money rolled in at an alarming rate.

The thing that did not arrive was a solution to Sid Millar's problem.

'*The Reflection* will rise to the challenge of rabbits' ears,' Mr Pottle thundered. 'Assemble a research team, Mr Tuohy. Institute a factory if necessary. We're going to show the nation how to make rabbits' ears that Britain can be proud of!'

Tuohy rang the educational hobbies shop that was run by a homosexual scoutmaster. 'We've still got those pictures from the 1965 Summer Camp, Mr Cuthbertson,' he coaxed.

'What do you want?'

'Tell me how to turn a plaster rabbit out of a mould without breaking the ears.'

'Oh, my God, Mr Tuohy, you have me there. An age-old problem, ears. Have you thought of trying gnomes?'

'Try 'em yourself,' Tuohy said and hung up.

At first George thought the small knot of people at the garden gate had come to admire his early showing of flowering cherry. By the time he had tidied himself to meet them the group had assumed crowd proportions. 'There he is!' cried a lady in a headscarf. She was pointing to Hilda's father who stood by his earless rabbits waving to his fans.

George listened to the sound of his own brains boiling. He reached for a garden rake and charged at the crowd. Just before it dispersed, shrieking, an impudent boy held aloft the morning's copy of *The Reflection*. '*The Bunnies that Bug Britain*' ran the banner headline.

When the people had departed George found that he was pointing the rake at his father-in-law. Sid grinned toothlessly. 'They're tlort of ditlinctive all the tlame,' he mused, in regard to his rabbits. 'Either they go or you do,' George hissed. 'If I go you won't get any of my money,' Sid said. 'Money, my eye!' fumed George. 'No,' Sid corrected mildly. 'My ears.'

Hilda and Edith were sorry about Sid's departure. George combed the whole of his garden meticulously to rid it of paw prints. *The Reflection* was ecstatic. That picture of the bent old figure of Sid Millar leaving home with one small suitcase and twenty plaster rabbits had to be the circulation clincher of the year. Mr Pottle called for Tuohy at home at an early hour to take him to a news stand. 'I want you to witness a sellout, m'boy,' he said, clapping him on the back so that the miserable little figure almost disintegrated. 'I want you to be the first man on the scene at the massacre of *The Moon*.'

The queue at the stand certainly was spectacular. 'Brilliant! Bloody brilliant!' Tuohy cackled as the happy citizens carried off their tabloids. They reached the stand in time to see a pensioner pounce on the last copy of . . . *The Moon*.

At least half the morning's quota of *The Reflection* remained in the racks. Pottle drew himself up to his full height and terrorized the senior citizen. 'Give me that, you ungrateful old garbage,' he bellowed, snatching the newspaper.

The front page of *The Moon* featured a four-column picture of Sid Millar with one arm around an achingly delicious Bunny Girl. With his free hand he was tweaking one of her fuzzy rabbit's ears. The paper, which told Sid's story in full while announcing his engagement to the eighteen-year-old beauty, shamelessly employed the catchline 'Souven-ear Issue'. Inside was a four-page picture supplement featuring pensioner Sid with his bride-to-be in a variety of costumes that ought to have been kept until after the ceremony.

The idea of actually proposing to Bonita Higglesworth had come to Sid when she was perched on his knee with no clothes on. It was a landscape of pink perfection. Her breasts were scoops of peach ice-cream; her knees, apricots. Her ears were like wafers of coral. You couldn't put a woman out in the garden for an ornament, of course, or sit her on the mantel-shelf like a clock.

You could look at her. Sid did, thinking how her cheeks would bulge like pillows when she was eating chocolate, how her amber eyes would melt while counting money, how delicately her lips would dip into a gin and orange: something that might be his; something that was perfect.

'Ummm, ummm, would you marry me?' he said.

Miss Higglesworth giggled. 'What 'ave you got to offer me?'

'I have got,' Sid said, 'twenty plaster rabbits – some of them are very good; fifty thousand pounds from the "Quid for Sid" fund and several terminal diseases.'

'I do,' Miss Higglesworth said, protruding her lips in a manner that caused two young photographers to faint.

'Exceptional,' Sid Millar wheezed.

Married

Mrs Hamilton is crying. Jack, who knows he is responsible because he is the only one there, says 'sorry'. He shrinks from her bunched-up shape and rolls on to a strange patch of the bed. The sawing noise that she makes with her tears will be heard in the other rooms. 'Shut up,' he says, but only in his head. Mrs Evans, the girl cyclists, Mrs Sargent and her daughter, they'll be awake by now; that nice couple, Jordan, the ornithologists.

In the lounge after tea they had sat on the blue banquette. There was a hole in their conversation. They smiled with their aching white faces. They eagerly discussed an ugly ashtray. The vividness of the day had eaten into them. The people who winked and wept and made speeches no longer had anything to do with their lives. They might have been pulled down and burnt like Christmas decorations.

The Jordans came into the lounge, both walking in that silent, loping manner developed for the stalking of mallards. They sat themselves down and introduced one another – Maud, Clement. Jack gave his name solemnly. He placed a hand on the arm of the girl beside him. It was a thin arm and beige, very soft, a child's limb. Flesh of his flesh. 'This is Mrs Hamilton,' he said in an offhand manner. He stroked that thin arm with the tips of his fingers. He was acquainted by heart with her hands and arms, her neck, the complicated little pathways of her ears. He knew nothing of the body that was slumped under careless clothes. He could only imagine. His fingers had often brushed the cloth of her dress where it was pushed by her figure and his breath had caught. He hardly dared to think about the rest of it but she always said it would be all right when they were married.

'It used to be a game preserve,' Maud Jordan said. She was speaking of the resort. 'This part of the beach is artificial. It came as a shock to us but it's a home from home now and there's life still in the grasses.'

She told the Jordans about their room with the huge wardrobe and the view of the sea. They said: 'The sea! Oh! Your room is next to ours.' They all seemed pleased about this as though it presented possibilities for a midnight feast. Jack could not concentrate. Having allowed his mind to run on he was unable to bring it back. The Jordans wanted to buy drinks. He could not attend to their demand for him to make a choice. He was filled with her fairness, the delicate waves of yellow hair, her soft face; grey eyes, gentle, under thick, assertive eyebrows. The wife. For the first time he realized that it was really so.

All day he had been trying to make it real. In the taxi on the way to church he had been clammy with the certainty that she would not turn up for she was careless about appointments. He concentrated on his mother's offended bulk, her head aimed out the window like a cannon of war under a bowl of pink net. 'There she is!' his mother cried out when the car pulled up at the gates. Her voice was triumphant as if she had spotted a criminal trying to get away.

When he looked at her in her white suit and the little round white hat his heart dwindled to nothing. She was too good for him. He did not deserve to hold a candle to her.

The wedding party went on all day. He sat at a long table next to his mother drinking beer and sherry and white wine, his jaw trembling and his eyes boiling away to navy points while he watched her dragged around the floor, tacked on to an assortment of men. She glowed for them as if she was in love. There was nothing he could do. He had no sense of ownership. He kept thinking of her voice, when she had accepted him for better or worse, as if someone had asked her did she smoke cigarettes. 'I do,' she agreed indifferently.

'Your husband!' Mrs Jordan was pressing. 'His mind's gone on holidays? What's he drinking?' The two women laughed in conspiracy over the foolishness of men. His spirits rose. He had been pushed into the ranks whereby women finally include men by taking them for granted. She turned to smile on him with the affectionate contempt of long-married wives. He swelled with confidence.

'Come along, Mrs H.,' he said, grasping her shoulder. 'Time for bed.' She looked at him in astonishment. The Jordans were still talking about their birds. 'Been a long day!' he reasoned. Jordan looked at him sharply as they said good-night.

He put his arm around her on the way up the stairs. 'They were nice,' he said; 'a nice married couple.' 'They were offended,' she said. 'You were rude to them. You never waited for the drinks.'

When they entered the gaunt pink room together he felt as pleased as he had ever been in his life. He switched on a lamp at the bedside. It was shaped like a doll. The pink gauze shade was some sort of ballet frock. It cast a healthy pink glow over the furniture. They had left their nightwear folded on the pillows and this was reassuring, his striped pyjamas, new, and her long night-dress with flowers. Hers did not look new, not even newly washed. After the momentary alarm when he had watched her taking it out of her case and noted this flaw he felt endeared by her lack of self-awareness.

She went over to the window and stood with her arms folded looking out at the sea which was the speckled silver of a fish. 'I want to tell you something,' she said, not turning around. 'Oh?' He felt the same stab. Why was it part of his nature always to fear the worst? 'What is it, love?' He undid his cuff links and laid them on the glass surface of the dressing-table. She shrugged. 'I want you to know something about me, who I am.' He smiled, relieved, and went to her. 'Who are you, then? Out with it? Mata Hari?' He wrapped his arms around her. She remained looking out to sea, her face, moon-pale, without a trace of a smile. 'You're my wife,' he said gently. 'That's all that matters to me.'

He went to the bathroom with his towel and his pyjamas neatly folded over his arm. He scrubbed his teeth and put talc on his hands to lessen their roughness. When he returned he was freshly bathed and angular in factory-ironed pyjamas. The hair at the back of his neck was damp and curling from the bathwater and he smelled of talcum powder.

She sat in a chair at the dressing-table. She was wearing her crumpled night-dress. Her face was still smeared with traces of lipstick and powder and she had not unpacked her toilet bag at the sink. He thought; she hasn't even bothered to brush her teeth. Each time a criticism of her came into his mind it was swept away by waves of love. She had her bare feet curled around the bar under the chair. She looked about ten. He went to her, his mind busy with thoughts of making her happy. He stroked her hair, her neck, her little pink ears. He felt covertly the throat of her nightie, the back, the sleeves. It was long. It hadn't the routine fastenings. He could find no approach. 'I'm tired,' she protested. He stroked her back to soothe her. She was stiff as a board. 'We won't do anything tonight,' she said.

He was disappointed. It was the way she said it, critical. She had a slight frown. She wouldn't look at him. He realized now that he had known it all along, that sort of behaviour wasn't on. Marriage didn't make it different.

He was resigned to leaving it, just holding her in his arms. He inched against her and took her into a rigid embrace. It was lovely to be cushioned on her chest. He freed one hand to feel, under cotton, her breasts. She sighed. He took his hand away. He put it on her hip as if they were dancing but when she moved away his fingers slipped and felt the rasp of hair through cloth. His hand came into contact with his own sexual self. It had grown and grown against the once-removed touch of her body and now it seemed to be all there was of him. He himself, that ordinary self who would have sacrificed all to make her happy, was shrinking away to nothing.

'Come to bed, now,' he begged.

'We haven't talked,' she said. 'It doesn't feel right.'

'Of course it's right,' he said doubtfully. 'You're my wife.'

She gave him a look of unhappy bewilderment. It shocked him to the core. It was plain that he was at fault although they had spoken all along of how happy they would be.

The prospect of being a good husband had been an ennobling one. She had taken it away from him. His desire for her was terrible. Trembling, he took the sides of her nightgown in bunched fists and pulled it up. Her white thighs were revealed and her sandy hair. She looked away modestly as if it was someone else's body. He thrust himself at her, his big redness which he hated. He pulled at her buttocks as if trying to separate the segments of an orange. He moved his hand between her legs and his fingernails scraped her flesh. He pushed a finger into the inside of her body. 'Cunt,' he said. 'Cunt! cunt!' He was astonished that she did not strike his face. He was trying to connect her sexual parts with the rudeness he associated with his own. All this exploring finger could think was, what an unprotected place. She did not make a sound. She moved away and he thought she was trying to escape from him. He would have let her go.

She lay down on the bed and pulled her knees up to her chin. She parted her legs. Her grey eyes were open, focussed on the ceiling, her face as polite as if she was arranging herself on a sofa. She pulled at the distant hem of her nightwear, gathering it in careful folds until it was over her knees. He felt foolish, standing there, watching her make a show of herself. It would be different if they were properly in bed.

He could not take his eyes off her red centre blazing in its twiggy-looking nest of hair. It was odd on such a pastel-coloured woman. He wanted to feel once more his manly custody of her frailty but the way she showed herself, like a prostitute, made him mad. He flung himself upon her and stabbed at her again and again, not caring if he hurt her, not wondering at her deadness. He felt no love for her, no pity. He reeled and skidded to his consummation. His tiny noise was loud against her silence.

He is cold. He is very tired. He is back again. The other Jack, the mad Jack, has gone, leaving him with the guilt. He is altogether to blame.

She pulls her nightie back down to her toes and draws her knees up under her. He can feel for her now. It's the man who is responsible. He ought to have been able to do better. In time he will make it up to her. At the moment he is ghostly with weariness.

He stands up from the bed and quenches the pink light from the ballet dancer's skirt. He has never seen anything so ugly. He goes back to her and strokes the stubborn lump of her shoulders. He picks her up from the surface of the bed. Her body remains clenched. He shoves the blankets back with his toes and lays her on the sheet with effort. Her un-yielding weight gives him a mirthful moment and he sniggers unwisely. 'Regular sack of hammers,' his mother used to say if he brought home a girl whom she considered more hefty than ladylike.

She makes a little cry of protest and her head struggles on the pillow although he is no longer holding her. She starts to cry. He draws back in dread of the jagged noises that are torn from her. He thinks of the Jordans sitting up in their room next door saying to each other that they didn't like the look of him – poor girl – should they knock?

'Sorry,' Jack says. She cannot hear him. She is boxed into her lament. 'Stop that now,' he says, a grumpy husband. She stops. She sniffs back her grief with a rude child's noise. She covers her ruined eyes with her fists. 'I wanted to tell you something,' she whimpers. He turns away from her. He is afraid of what she is going to say. 'It doesn't matter,' he says. 'We're starting fresh.'

He is very tired. He keeps thinking that there is something he has forgotten and then, as his brain starts to slip away he remembers, oh yes, he forgot to kiss her.

'When I was nine,' she says, 'my mother sent me to buy a hen. I carried it home under my arm and it went to the toilet in the pocket of my blazer. A new blazer, eucalyptus green! She never laid any eggs. She used to sit on the front step and wait for people to come out and stroke her on the head.'

'I'll never understand her,' he thinks quite rightly, trying to bash a serviceable dent with his head in the unfamiliar pillow; 'not if I live to be a hundred.'

Lying down on a pillow next to hers, he feels much better. Their heads, precisely arranged, like earrings in a box, are very married. Boldly he reaches out for her hand. 'Well, missus,' he says. 'We're well and truly wedded now. Well, Mrs Hamilton?'

A Reproduction

Some people shouldn't be given reproduction equipment, but it's standard issue. Ladies are like window boxes, painted and shallow and open to the elements. Men, like colds, are catching.

'Stop me,' he smiled.

'It's quite safe,' I smiled. 'The seventeenth is the day.'

'I really think you've got it all wrong,' he smiled.

When I found I was pregnant I didn't tell my husband right away; none of his business since it probably wasn't his.

'Stop me,' teased my lover.

'It's all right,' I smiled. 'I'm pregnant.'

One smile too many and they were all gone. My lover turned into a pillar of salt. I myself was more like a little glass dish of salt on a boarding-house table, weeping copiously because I had not been stopped.

He spoke through the sheets like an obscene telephone caller. 'We'll get you an abortion.'

'I want my child,' I sniffed.

'You told me I was all you wanted,' he warned.

'Abortions are dangerous,' I sobbed.

'Less dangerous than childbirth and you've already been spared the hazards of the Pill,' spoke the sheets, reckless now and veering perilously close to logic.

'I know all about those lunch-time abortions with doctors in crimson aprons and screams from the incinerator,' I wept.

'It's twenty-four hours with a full English breakfast.'

I threw up and felt I had had the final throw.

When I told my husband he went off to commit suicide. In the gas oven or the tallest tree, he met Anthea. She came home and started scrubbing his wronged underwear before I had packed my cases. I found her sitting by the fire drinking a tumbler of the whisky I only got when I had a cold. She put another log in my open brick fireplace and grinned at me through long, white teeth. 'Made a frightful hash of things, haven't you?' she said amiably.

I moved in with my lover, creaking with condemned pride and trying desperately to appear healthy, like a pensioner going to live with the marrieds.

There are manuals filled from cover to cover with excuses for husbands. Every girl knows that husbands suffer from sexual fatigue, go prematurely bald, forget birthdays and prefer their mothers' cooking. Lovers are to be found only in romantic fiction as dark maned, well hung, square jawed, with burning eyes and no relatives, permanently erect and permanently smiling.

He wore nylon socks. He liked warm milk with his cornflakes. His hair was shaped with hairspray and his face was cast with gloom.

'Perhaps it won't be too bad, darling,' I said, running my knitting needles through his hair. A face filled with dread floated into my vision, like a spectre in a nightmare. 'It will be a tiny, blue-eyed intellectual. We'll feed it sieved smoked salmon and red wine in a plastic bottle.'

'It's still there, then?' he said.

Anthea opened the door to me when I arrived with my suitcase. 'Oh, I say!' she greeted. 'How many of you are there?' My husband bounded forward looking scrubbed and mischievous, like a schoolboy in an advertisement. I moaned piteously; 'Take me back.' The three of us trooped into the living room which was transformed with macramé and little fat candles as ugly as toads. 'Have a drink,' Anthea said, waving the whisky. 'Oh, golly, sorry – I forgot.' She filled herself a quarter pint and sat back, waiting.

I addressed myself to my husband. 'I can't live without you, I'm so miserable I could die. I love you.' My tears volleyed like angry little pellets into the calm silence. I opened one flooded eye and could see a brown-suited swimmer, smiling.

'No you don't,' he said agreeably. 'Not at all.'

He made tea. It was good tea. I hadn't had a good cup of tea in ages. We sat around the fire eating Anthea's awful oatmeal biscuits and talking about her nerves. 'I wouldn't know sleep if it sat on my face,' she said. I congratulated her and said goodbye. I hadn't stood a chance. My nerves were weighted down with hormones.

When I got back my lover was reading a book. A pink puppet reared up above the literature and bowed to me. It was his hand, clothed in one of the tiny pink dresses I had been knitting, absurdly small for a human being. My heart leaped. He was waving to me in greeting. He was reading Dr Spock.

'Girls,' he said, 'are more intelligent than boys up to the age of nine years.'

'I didn't know you cared,' I said.

'You didn't tell me it was going to be a girl.'

I came over and hid my mouth in his hair. He patted my behind with a big hand innocent in pink drag. We put away the knitting and the reading and went to the bedroom holding hands. It was a long time since I had undressed in the middle of the day. 'I'm a whale,' I giggled. 'A meringue,' he contradicted elegantly.

'Stop me,' he said suddenly.

I sat up. 'It's all right . . .'

'Dr Spock disagrees with excessive physical contact.'

'But that's for parents and children,' I argued.

'I know,' he frowned. 'That's what I mean.'

*

It was a boy. I apologized profusely but there was nothing I could do. The nurse slapped it to cover its screams and then washed it in cold water like a fish and placed it, floundering, on my chest. In many ways it was a better person than I. Its face was a squint of honest malice while I was still trying to smile. It understood its role more than I did mine. While I was trying to pluck the little pink leech from my breast it stopped howling and drew the furious wet cavity of its mouth into an amazed 'o' which it clamped on to the cotton over my flesh.

'He wants to feed,' the nurse said.

I was paralysed by its lack of modesty.

'You specified breastfeeding,' she prompted.

I remained rigid, as in a nightmare where one finds oneself in bed with one's boss. The nurse schluk-schlukked swiftly across the floor in determined canvas shoes. She jerked at the ribbon of my nightie and pulled out a breast which she plugged into the child. I felt as if I had been caught hoarding beneath my clothing something not rightfully mine.

It was a relief, all the same, that the business had begun. Its urgent, predatory kiss was all at odds with the vulnerable, feathery feel of its body and it hurt me, like an inconsiderate man, but it forced me to think of it as a person. There were moments when I felt I could be drawn into the marshy world of motherhood. It made little squeaks of bliss while it fed and I was grateful someone was pleased with me.

'Sorry,' I said again, catching sight of my lover who had sat there through it all, breathing in and out and bearing down.

His face was appalled, as if it had been stretched on a last, far out of proportion to my perfectly human error in having got the wrong number of chromosomes into the recipe. His eyes pierced my peculiar little pink gentleman; his horror was woven into the child. For the first time I, too, looked directly at my baby, but defensively, to counter the evil eye.

I searched the small, fussy face which was red as a rasher

and furrowed as a waffle. It seemed that in his first few minutes he had already been stamped with an identity. He looked . . . like all other babies, for goodness' sake.

'He looks,' said my lover, digging up my thought, solicitous as a dog, 'exactly like your husband.'

I did my best. I defy anyone to say otherwise. I called him Julian although the name sat as awkwardly on his angry florid form as did the crochet bonnet I tied on to disguise his lingering alopecia. When I brought him home I put him in a fashionable wooden cradle, hung about with ethnic mobiles. I dyed the pink dresses purple, which seemed a creative compromise between pink and blue. Yet he was not the best of company. He belched and scowled and bellowed like a scoundrel. Sleep was nowhere among his skills. All night there was the grizzled thread of reproach so full of misery that it drove us grown-ups to opposite edges of our bed lest our comfort deprive him of the full complement of our futility.

His demands for food were a Wagnerian opera and he cunningly adjusted his appetites nightly so that I could not anticipate his needs and leap to his side, bare-breasted, a Wagnerian offering, before the storm broke.

The storm broke after six months. My lover and I sat in the kitchen looking like death, sharing breakfast with the cautious concentration of famine victims. We ate, quickly, furtively, hunched up against the onslaught of the monotonous music of human wrath.

When the singing started, we leaped up and began running in different directions, rescuing bottles from the sterilizing unit not inaptly called 'Milton' (for who, more than new parents, understands about paradise lost). We mixed formulas to a consistency of wet cement. It was eight seconds or so before we realized that the sound was the telephone. 'Thought we'd just drop round and say "hi" to the little home-wrecker,' Anthea boomed. Did she mean me or the baby? 'Ten minutes, say. Good-o.' She hung up. I hadn't said a single word.

We might have moved house or anything. She could have been speaking to a perfect stranger.

I dropped the speaking set and scurried about the house gathering to myself a small community of colouring agents and camouflages. 'Not for you,' I said ruefully as I collided with my face in a bathroom mirror.

They arrived on the dot and stood bouncing like yo-yos behind the glass door panel and pressing the bell. The noise set the baby howling. Their shining good health and good spirits were an intrusion on our chaos. Anthea savoured the screams, the spilt feeding mixture, our faces as dim and grey as pillow covers in tenements. 'So,' she said; 'this is where the other thing gets you.'

'This,' said my lover, speaking for the first time in months, 'has nothing at all to do with the other thing.'

At the sight of Anthea looming over his crib, the baby stopped crying and assumed a coy expression that made him look, under mountains of lacy knitting, like a bridal gnome. I had covered most of his face with a bonnet and powdered his shiny pink cheeks for a disguise. Anthea was studying him oddly. She deftly polished his cheek with a thumb and it showed russet like a pomegranate.

With a twitch, she deprived him of his pixie. An army of orangey hairs crept up the back of his neck and over his skull to a point quite near his forehead – the point, in fact, to which my husband's orangey hair had retreated.

'I *say*,' she said.

I went for a long walk after they took him. It wasn't regret, exactly, but just as Anthea settled him into the car for the first time in his life, he smiled. I felt an awful twinge as I recognized that smile. There was surely no mistaking that smile. 'Stop me,' he seemed to say to me, as he betrayed me.

He still has that smile except when he shows those long white teeth that make him look so like Anthea, when he grins with delight and says: 'Tell me, auntie! Tell me about the man with the hairspray.'

When I got back there was no one there. All his clothes were gone, nothing left of him except his note. 'Gone forever,' he wrote. 'I lived for that child.'

Not a Recommended Hobby
for a Housewife

Poor Maria. She had gone to seed.

The girls kissed her, assessed her savagely and then bent with uniform delicacy to their meal of omelette with salad and a dry white wine. But the message had been transmitted, processed. She was late. She was getting fat. She was wearing, for God's sake, a fur coat with jeans.

The girls were all in their thirties; a good age, because their faces had not yet fallen apart; a bad age, because their dreams had. Twenty years ago they had been friends at school. They met once a year for lunch. They were conscientious about the reunion. It brought the years together and smoothed them over, keeping youth in view and disappointment in hand. Plotting one another's failings with monstrous efficiency, they could each tell that their own lives were not wholly unsuccessful.

Elizabeth had got herself a job. 'Well, I had to, damn it,' she said, defending herself against a lack of response. 'The truth is, my Morgan has become a stinge.'

Maria ordered herself a lobster whose death had been ritualized in cream and cheese and brandy, and then recklessly demanded a bottle of red wine.

'It isn't as if we're poor,' said Elizabeth, dragging back the attention of Helen and Joan who had been temporarily dazed by the sheer tastelessness of poor Maria. 'We've been doing frightfully well since Morgan got his award in Vienna. I mean, he buys me stuff all right.' She shook wrists weighted down with lumps of gold and surveyed her jewelled fingers. 'It's just that he won't actually give me money.'

It was impossible to ignore the stones on her hands. They were like traffic lights. She did not permit herself to look at her friends directly but concentrated on her fingers, hoping to catch in the gleaming gems a reflection of the precise moment when sympathy gave way to ...

Cruelly, she cut short her own pleasure. 'I like working,' she pronounced. 'I like having my own money. And it isn't really like work, putting down names and dates in a diary and making occasional cups of coffee.' She laughed lightly. 'The hardest thing is getting used to another man's moods.'

The hardest thing, Maria had found, was getting used to another man's shape. Over ten years she had geared herself to an armful of hostile, nervous bones that had to be gathered together with perseverance and tamed with authority before they could be melted down for honey. Harry was so relaxed he covered her like a sauce and she needed his erection, not just for sex, but because she expected something aggressive in the shape of a man.

The other thing was the response. Searching for her orgasm in the smiling dark, Maria was totally unprepared for a strange man's voice in her ear. 'Is it good? Isn't it wonderful?' She had opened her eyes and the man moving over her seemed as remote as if she was looking out of a window at a child skipping in the street.

Harry had never been married, of course. People who had been married for a time did not expect things to be wonderful. They were even irritated by wonder, like old folk blinking crossly in bright sunlight.

She herself was not totally innocent of wonder. That was in the past. She saw herself in her mind's eye, not just younger, but smaller, a scale model, working away at the orange Formica counter with the aid of a fiendish cookbook. Perfectly good pieces of rib steak had been buried in a snowstorm of coconut, curry-powder, tinned fruit – even dried prunes once. 'Is it good?' she would beg, as Ned obediently forked the sludge into his mouth.

Ned, in bed, had massaged all the wrong places and then speared her with the single-mindedness of a Kamikaze. 'Is it good?' he would demand.

'Wonderful, wonderful,' they each assented, as though wonder waited just around the corner and could be lured into their lives by mere encouragement.

'Wonderful! Simply wonderful!' Helen was talking about her hobby. She had taken up Origami. It sounded like an unnatural act, she admitted with a gay little giggle but was, in fact, the art of folding paper.

Elizabeth and Joan exchanged the briefest of glances. Definitely an unnatural act, signalled the demurely dancing lashes.

'The Japanese do it,' Helen explained.

'What *don't* the Japanese do?' Joan said.

'Just ordinary paper. John says that our town alone throws out two hundred tons of waste paper a year. He's into re-cycling now. He's such a vital person. He really keeps you on your toes. I don't mind admitting I had begun to mope a bit when Jeff – the baby – brought home a girl last year. "Get yourself a hobby, Helen," John said. "Don't get on my back."' Her lips shivered. She picked up a paper napkin and began tearing at it with such nervous determination that for an instant the others experienced compassion.

It was a paper bird, tiny and perfect, so thin that the yellow smoky light of the restaurant shone right through. Such a bird might perch on a Perilla tree to bathe in the curious hay scent and sing the praises of a smoky-yellow Eastern dawn. The women were silent. They knew a redemption when they saw one.

The mood lasted a moment or two. Maria's meal arrived. The lobster seemed to throb with sensual energy although in fact it was just the cream and cheese still whispering from the grill. Maria gulped her wine like a mug of milk. She gouged out a piece of lobster and bit it. It was murderously delicious.

Joan watched her warily, her mouth a mere scar of invisible mending. Her eyes crept back to the bird, cradled in the branches of a hand that was unconsciously closing. 'Hobbies are fine in their own way,' she said like a ventriloquist, with no perceptible lip movement. 'But they don't fulfil you as a person.'

Of all of them, Joan had improved most over the years. She had changed from a plain girl into a stylish woman. She was marvellously thin and expensively beige and was sculpted into a pale grey suit from France and a cream cashmere sweater. She looked, Maria thought, like a tasteful piece of modern pottery. She did not look, they all thought, fulfilled as a person.

'Don't laugh now, girls, but I've been getting into charity work,' she said. They did not laugh. They beamed; Joan making stuffed dates for sales of work and buns for functions!

'Snacks on tracks – that sort of thing?' Helen scratched a piece of lettuce around in a pool of lemon dressing.

'Meals on wheels,' Joan corrected. 'That and visiting lonely old folk. I love it really and it's been *good* for me. It's only once a week. Wednesdays are my days.'

Wednesdays were Harry's days too. Ned had arranged that. 'Won't be home on Wednesdays from now on, my love,' he had said. Something about golf and a conference, she thought, but his voice had drowned in the depths of her boredom. She found Harry in an art gallery and went home with him.

She liked his brown bachelor flat with its full bottles of whisky and wine. She liked his short toenails and his exotic smell and how he didn't keep looking in ovens and fridges to check on what was there that had not been there before, like a husband. She liked not having to make the bed afterwards.

The women called for coffee and a truce. Year by year they became more uneasy in each other's company, more anxious to call the meeting to order. There was nothing that wouldn't keep for another year. Then Maria ordered Black Forest cake. 'What have you been doing with yourself, darling?' Elizabeth asked in tones that were unnecessarily harsh. Maria shrugged. 'Oh, this and that. Nothing much. I'm afraid I'm not energetic like the rest of you.' 'It's time you took your life in hand.' Elizabeth shook a fork at her. 'In no time at all the children will be gone and you'll be middle-aged. You have to think ahead.'

The cake was brought – damp brown sponge breathing fumes of Kirsch with slovenly piles of whipped cream sliding down the sides; big, wet, crimson cherries sank into the snow-drift under a hail of chocolate curls. Maria stuck her fork into the cake – a gesture that herded her friends to the edge of outrage. 'I hate to have to say it,' Elizabeth said, 'but you've let yourself go.'

Maria accepted the reproach and put it away like a precious gift. It was true. She had let herself go.

It had been Tuesday, not Wednesday. The doctor told her she had to have a hysterectomy and she stepped out of his surgery and into a downpour, letting the rain wash all over her so that she might weep unobserved. It wasn't that she wanted another baby but it seemed such a miserable thing, to have the middle torn out of one's body. She felt old and disposable. She phoned Ned and a girl said that he was in conference.

She stood in the rain for a full ten minutes until her flat leather, bad-weather shoes filled with water and her costly curls lay on her forehead like torpid worms. She thought of Harry. It was not Wednesday but surely he existed on other days. She knew that he painted his strange purple pictures at home and that home was comfortingly nearby.

Maria knocked on Harry's door. 'It's open,' he said. She

stepped inside and stood there, passive and dismal, puddles of water hanging at her feet.

Harry was propped up in bed eating a cheese sandwich, toasted. He wore a vest which matched his greying sheets and he hadn't shaved in days. 'What do you want?' he said. His look was a mixture of accusation and horror, which hurt until she realized she was looking at him in the same way. The thought struck them mutually so that they each cringed as though naked, although naked they had rather flaunted. 'You've never come on Tuesday before,' he said. 'My cleaner comes on Wednesday morning.' Maria wondered if the cleaner dumped him in the tub, leaving him to soak while she set about changing the bed and cleaning the flat.

Her own explanation, she realized as she said it, was just as irrelevant. 'I've got to have a hysterectomy.' She was surprised all the same when he started to laugh. It began as a slow, unshaven-man's chuckle, deep in his belly. 'I'm sorry, lady,' he finished up bellowing. 'I'm not a doctor.'

She marched over to the bed, still dripping, seized him by the shoulder and hit him. His laughter stopped, cut off at the mains. He pulled her on to the bed and pranced upon her, his body a primitive implement of conquest. He kissed her. She bit his mouth. He sank his teeth into her ear and then tore off her clothes to find more vulnerable places upon which to put punishment. He scrubbed down and up the length of her body with his unshaven face and they glared into each other's eyes with malice. There was no distance between them. No one else existed in the world. Her condemned womb lurched defiantly. 'I love you,' she said. 'I love you,' he said.

They never noticed part of a toasted cheese sandwich somewhere in there with them; never even noticed wonder when it found them, limp and aimlessly optimistic amid the greying sheets, like the cloth toys of a child.

Maria licked. The last morsels of cream and crumbs

vanished from her fork. The others hovered, solicitous in their awe, to make sure it had all been eaten.

They were the only women in the restaurant who didn't notice a handsome man walk in alone. When Harry reached the table Maria already had an arm stretched outward to close the gap between them. She looked at him with eyes that said it all. Her lover.

His full credentials could only be guessed: that he would sweep her face with his hair to dry her tears or bring tears to her eyes; that he would nourish her breasts with his kisses; that he was brave enough to enter the place that had been vandalized by children and was due to be demolished.

Maria stood, aided by her lover's hand. Harry signalled for a bill and took it. The girls gaped, ungainly and timid as the children they had once been together.

'Next year,' Maria said, smiling.

'Next year!' they echoed, grasping adjective and noun as they began to slide back into the chasm of their lives.

A Nail on the Head

On several evenings in the year Benjamin Hart brings home people to his wife. They are for dinner. The characters belong to the life he leads between outward- and homeward-bound trains. He assembles them with care and selflessly – a good assortment; wit and distinction, pretty faces and ones that have been photographed for the newspapers, the occasional homosexual or journalist. The people are not vital to his situation in life. They have not stretched his talents or contributed to the bulk of his pocket. He chooses them for Mirabel. On these occasions his wife wears a long green dress that she has had for many years and puts upon the table items in aspic and troublesome puddings supported with eggs. It is very nice.

To understand Benjamin's solicitude it is necessary to know about Mirabel. She is thirty but has withstood cellulite (Benjamin is unclear about cellulite but imagines it as a form of breakfast cereal harmful to the intestines).

Her face is free of flaws. She read in a magazine article that crumpling of the eye tissue could be forestalled by smiling with an outward curve rather than an upward one. She practised this in a mirror and now produces a smile so strained and frugal that people imagine it has to do with sex. In fact her passion is invested mainly in the stripping and re-covering of old furniture. Mirabel is a skilled housewife. She renders down the tailbones of beasts into delicious stews and cakes of jellied meat. She does not work in a job. She does not demand children. In spite of the fact that she once went to the university where she read Medieval English, she never complains. Benjamin believes that this is because he has not increased her housekeeping allowance in keeping with the cost of living, nor his own substantial increments. She runs the household wonderfully on a modest budget. It extends her capabilities.

Benjamin once heard a woman complain about being left to rot in the house. It haunted him. There was a suggestion of wastefulness, as if some perfectly good leftover had been neglected in the fridge until disfigured by invading organisms.

He made up his mind that it would never happen with Mirabel. It was a problem. Although he did not wish her to rot in the house, he could not countenance the idea of her gadding about outside, prey to the corruption of the world beyond. Owing to the pressure of his work, he had very little to do with her. He often mentioned her, though, when people complained about the state of things. 'My wife ...' he would impress, offering a point about her skill with over-ripe tomatoes, her stand against cellulite. They all agreed that she sounded a marvel. They clamoured to meet her. This was how Benjamin hit on the idea. He would bring Mirabel company. She would enjoy the fruit of his social labours, the pick of the crop. He felt he had hit the nail on the head.

The Harts live in a house which is called 137. A new road veers muddily out of the town, found hoarding a plot of ground behind an oldish council estate. Two hundred red-brick houses were crammed into this space. The buildings pursue a series of small zig-zagging roads as though fleeing in panic from the bulldozers that rumbled into the ground for a year.

In fact this apparently meaningless pattern was the ingenious design of an architect, facilitating the intrusion of five extra houses. The residents, having a homing instinct, do not notice, but it confounds the logic of the numbers. Visitors and debt-collectors can be seen swerving their cars out of different cul-de-sacs well into the night. A series of false trails leading to 137 is particularly cunning. On previous occasions there have been guests lacking in persistence who failed to locate it, leaving gaps like missing teeth in the evening. One fellow, knocking on a door to refresh his directions, had struck up an acquaintance with a perfect stranger and gone off with him for the night. Since then Benjamin has made a point of fixing a neutral place of assembly, usually the new cabaret lounge, with its myopic red sign blinking over the town. He allows his guests to purchase a round apiece to work themselves up into a party spirit, so that by the time he leads them back to Mirabel they are, so to speak, at room temperature.

All the way to the pub he smiles at this piece of humour which he has just thought up. He would find it hard not to smile. Having just left his kitchen where little French beans gleam waxily like a pile of green crayons in the sink and ox kidneys on the stove succumb their toughness to a splash of Spanish brandy, his joy is large and assertive. He nestles between twin monuments. At home, beauty and thrift are testimony to his successful marriage. Two miles away, a knot of mildly successful people, petrified by strangeness, await his unifying phrase, his warming presence. He seeks nothing in return. Their very adherence to him will testify to his significance in the larger world, even though he hardly knows them.

Mirabel has bought a spray of lilac. It cost forty-five pence. It lies on the kitchen counter, swaddled in white like a baby, while she worries. For the same price she could have had a bunch of tulips, five or six in egg-yolk yellow or chilblain pink. They were not very nice but they had bulk on their side.

She fetches a decanter without a stopper. It was ten pence at a sale of work and she knew it would come in handy. She fills it with water and inserts the lilac. It lolls like a plume in an ink well. She carries this through to the lounge and puts it on a low coffee table which she herself lacquered in black. She sighs with relief. The single pinkish bloom flames like a candle, warming up the pale silky covering of the sofa. The money has not been wasted.

The sofa is old. Its cushions are filled with down. She bought it second-hand for fifty pounds and sewed the covers herself. The curtains are in a similar shade although they do not match. She had to do the best she could with what was in the sales. The walls are painted like the undersides of mushrooms and there is a rug of whitish animal hair on the floor. With a small fire in the grate and a dish of black olives gleaming on the black table, the room will look like one in a magazine.

From a cabinet in the lounge she fetches a decanter which has a stopper. From a bag advertising a supermarket, she withdraws a bottle of sherry. *Ernesto Sanchez* the label admits. It cost a pound and fifty pence. At the end it swarms like brown sugar in hot whisky.

She admires the components of the dinner, bathed in oil or cream and bursting with nutrition. The entire meal (excluding the wines, which Benjamin will carry home in a brown paper bag, not counting the expense) is costing less than five pounds. In spite of some inauspicious ingredients it will be delicious, even the cold rice pudding, boiled then frozen, then crowned with a plastic basket of strawberries and a French title. Mirabel would like to have the neighbours in, Mrs Stanley and Mrs Winter, to pick over her bargains and consolidate her achievement but she imagines in advance their resentment at not being compelled to take something more than a cerebral pleasure in her work. She contents herself with stealing one of the strawberries – her first of the season – and making a wish. 'I wish –', the thought rises like a wisp of smoke on her neat brain.

She does not wish for a better home or a new dress. She

does not even wish for a better sherry. She visits the rooms of her tranquil and economical home. She sighs, flops down into the sofa, rises upon hearing bashes of greeting on the front door, and repairs the small damage inflicted on her cushions by her bottom. She straightens her lips into a smile and hurries to the hall to welcome her guests, berating herself for foolish thoughts. After all the trouble she has gone to, it would be ridiculous to wish they weren't coming.

There stands on the doorstep a tall youth with shorn hair and rosy cheeks and a coarse-looking middle-aged woman in a fur coat. Between them is a child with short blonde hair and a pointy nose and in the background, a tall foxy woman, frozen into fashionable repose. Mirabel, standing on the warm side of the door, keeps her mouth rigid with welcome. She imagines that behind this group she sees a large dog and some-one draped like a towel over the fence. She is further confused when the boy with the rosy cheeks extends a big red hand and says: 'Hi, I'm Roxanne.'

There is a moment in which Mirabel thinks that they may be Jehovah's Witnesses or Friends of the Earth but then she sees Benjamin coming up the drive, bow-legged under a clank-ing brown paper bag, so she murmurs 'Do come in', and shrinks back into the hall.

They crowd into the living room and stand shouting out their names, further identifying themselves with occupations. The woman in the fur coat is called Norma. She writes for a newspaper. Roxanne, in spite of crew-cut and combat clothes, is a girl. Benjamin introduces her as an artist but she has already confided to Mirabel in the hall that she works as a char. The gnome turns out to be the same age as Mirabel. Her name is Flora and she says she is a seer. The tall fashionable woman is Sybil King. She makes dresses which sell for hundreds of pounds. 'And this is Lionel,' she says of the man around whose hips her fingers flutter. 'He does heads.' 'A sculptor!' cried Benjamin. Mirabel cannot give her attention. She is focussed on the man's pink jeans. She could swear she saw them hanging on her fence a few seconds earlier.

'He's a hairdresser,' Sybil says. 'Everyone goes to Lionel. He's divine.' Mirabel looks doubtful. 'He's a bit under the weather tonight,' Sybil explains. 'He's been mixing his drinkies. I'm afraid he had to have a little sicky outside but we made him lean over the fence into your neighbour's garden, didn't we, darling?' Lionel belches threateningly. His knees sag and he collapses into an armchair covered in oyster-coloured Dralon velvet. Mirabel watches his trembling lips in terror. She tries to think what she will say to Mrs Stanley in the morning about her begonias, shrivelled under Lionel's illness. Her concentration is damaged by a commotion in the hall. There is a sequence of gruff yelps and some language. An enormous dog, which she had earlier thought she saw in the garden, drags Benjamin into the living room on a lead. 'Sorry, dear,' Benjamin says as the dog grinds mud into the white rug. 'He's very strong.'

'Come to Mummie?' Sybil pats an arm of the sofa. The dog bounds over, scrabbling the silk with ferocious paws. 'She's a Borzoi,' Sybil boasts.

'What's her name?' Mirabel says in a high tone of voice.

'Lucrezia.'

After a silence there comes a high-pitched whinny of laughter which floats like a streamer over the room. The woman in the fur coat is pink in the face, gobbling with mirth. 'Lucrezia Borzoi,' she yelps. 'Oh, Jesus God, I'm going to have a heart attack.' Her body shakes as if inhabited by an unreliable engine and tears dribble down her bunched-up jowls.

'Pardon?' Sybil says.

Mirabel feels it is up to her. She grabs Norma by her furry shoulders and rattles her vigorously. 'Let me take your coat, please,' she says. But Norma will not let go her fur. Mirabel tugs at it a few moments more but Norma says no, she is cold, it cost three thousand pounds.

Mirabel offers her a glass of sherry to warm her up. 'Horse's wee-wee,' the woman laughs with contempt, before eagerly accepting.

In the kitchen Mirabel arranges the decanter of sherry on a round wicker tray with seven little matching glasses. The glasses are engraved with flowers. She bought eight of them so that she would not be heartbroken when one got broken. Her matched glasses, her perfect dinner, snoring in pots on the stove, lend her strength. She lifts the lids from saucepans and smiles at the contents as if they are children in prams. Mercifully, the smile stays in place as she seizes the tray and marches back to the lounge.

The guests have all found places to sit. The three women are on the sofa, the gnome is on a cushion on the floor. Lucrezia, the dog, lies in front of the fire, roasting her behind. Benjamin sits on the edge of a brittle Regency chair, studying Lionel for signs of life.

Crammed with people the room has taken heart. Mirabel notices a frill of Sybil's pleated chiffon dress fanning out around an edge of the sofa. She watches Flora's cap of yellow hair, nicely cut by some Lionel or other, and the neat lotus fold of her ankles on the cushion. She sees the bluish shimmer of Norma's fur and Lionel's handsome head flung back in the armchair. She feels a little thrill of pride. It is nice to have one's home filled with friends. She hands round the sherry, passing by Lionel's chair, but his hand shoots out and appropriates a glass with speed. She takes her own glass to the remaining armchair by the fire.

'Well, this is very nice, Harold,' Norma says when they are all settled. Mirabel looks up in surprise scanning the room for a new face, a Harold, but Norma has her eye on Benjamin. 'It's Benjamin,' Mirabel says. 'What's Benjamin?' Norma says eagerly. 'My husband's name is Benjamin,' Mirabel persists.

Norma looks at him with respect. 'Benjamin. I never thought of him as a Benjamin.'

'How did you meet him?' Mirabel says.

'D'you know, we've never actually met. We travel on the same train sometimes. He reads the back of my newspaper. Damned irritating habit.'

'He's a bit of a dark horse, our Benj,' Sybil says crossly. Mirabel is astonished. 'He never told me he had a wife tucked away in the suburbs.' 'Have you known him long?' says Mirabel. Sybil squints back into her memory. 'We met, oh, two, three years back. Your husband came into my shop and asked to see something for less than five pounds. "You can add two noughts to anything in my shop, dear," I told him. Quick as a flash he said: "Give me something with two knots for less than five pounds." I like a man with a sense of humour. I told him straight out. It's what makes a man sexy. I'll bet he's a rattler in the sack.'

'Three years,' says Mirabel faintly.

'That was the last I saw of him,' Sybil goes on; 'until last week when he walked into the shop, out of the blue and asked me to dinner. Mind you, this wasn't quite what I had in mind. You can bet your sweet bippy I wouldn't have worn a five-hundred-pound dress if I'd known we were going to wallow in the family trough.'

Mirabel feels dazed by all this talk of prices. She is used to discussing bargains with her neighbours. It is her favourite topic. Her mind cannot accommodate talk of hundreds and thousands. At least Roxanne is giving her no worry in that quarter. The girl, who appears to be falling asleep, is wearing clothes that must have come lately from a rubbish bin. She remembers her manners and is about to tell Sybil that it is a lovely dress but Norma rends the air with a shrill cry of triumph. 'Five hundred pounds? Well, *that's* a figure to impress. The dress is divine, darling. What a pity your ribs stick out more than your tits.'

Sybil frowns at Benjamin. 'You should have told me you were married, dear. It's a bit of luck I had old Lionel tagging along for a drink this evening, that's all I can say.' She stands up and picks cautious steps to where Lionel is sleeping. She falls heavily into his lap. 'I have lovely tits, don't I darling?' she says. She squirms her bottom in his crotch, disturbing the rhythm of his snoring.

Roxanne has been lustily eyeing the space on the sofa vacated by Sybil. 'Far out,' she says. She heaves her boots up on to the cushions. Clumps of mud scar the silk as she shuffles her legs to make herself comfortable. 'Dinner's ready,' Mirabel shouts.

It is a lovely dinner. Everyone says so: pools of green soup in white bowls, little rolls, home-made with milk and poppy-seed crusted. Benjamin measures yellow wine into their glasses and voices carve the air above the clash of spoons. Mirabel catches his eye. They smile at one another.

Everything has been towards this moment. Their home, the offspring of their endurance, has been kissed to life. They are accomplices, woven together with parental pride, aglow with reflected glamour. Her breasts shimmer beneath candle-light in the old green dress; his red silk handkerchief flares irresistibly in his worn corduroy jacket. The blurred, dancing edges of their smiles are a living, vital language, like the intricate frame of strange phrases that surrounds them and isolates them. The guests are on the outside. Eat, drink and be as merry as they may, they know they will be flung out into the cold before the night is over; and who can be absolutely sure that this scene does not continue forever inside the house, without them.

Mirabel asks Flora if she will always be happy, always have love. Flora, who now that she has a cushion on her chair and no one can see that her feet don't touch the ground, looks more normal than anyone, says: 'Oh, love, yes, that's no problem.' 'What do you mean?' the others clamour peevishly.

They are all, except Mirabel and Benjamin, on their own, are they not? And Roxanne's husband, the louse, did he not once try to strangle her?

'Anyone can have love,' Flora says. 'We've all got love. It's just a matter of making up our mind to the fact that it may never be returned.' Flora's face is pink and round. Her lips are moist. Her hair moves in a piece, shining gold. Although she is much less than five feet in height and probably tells fortunes behind a velvet curtain in a council flat, anyone can see that she is a person of quality, a priestess. They cannot hide their tawdry hearts. They make up for it by being pitifully good, eating all their bread, listening without interrupting.

'Love may not be mutual,' Flora says softly. 'It may not be rewarding. It may not even benefit the person at whom it is directed. But real love is indestructible.'

Mirabel thinks it is beautiful. She cannot imagine where this small, tidy, sensible person has been all her life. She is about to raise this point when she notices that the soup bowls are empty and that Norma has had time to smoke a whole cigarette and grind the stub into a green puddle of soup. She seizes this stinking arrangement and the other bowls and hurries to the kitchen to reinforce supplies.

When the main course is put on the table it appears to present a problem to Lionel. 'What are these?' he says, aiming his fork fuzzily at what look like a lot of very small boxing gloves in cream. 'Kidneys, dear,' Norma booms. 'Glandular organs for the excretion of urine.' 'God,' Lionel groans. He gazes on the kidneys reproachfully for a moment before bolting from the room. On his way through the lounge he leans against the wall and with an expression of surprise, vomits explosively over the white fur rug. Some of it, Mirabel notes, goes on the sofa. 'There, there, old man,' Benjamin cries out in alarm. He hurries into the lounge, closing over the folding doors so as not to offend the guests any more than is necessary, but after that none of them does more than toy with the meal. They eat the strawberries off the Riz à l'Impératrice and at last Mirabel is able to leave them with an excuse about grinding coffee. She does not grind coffee, nor even her teeth. She puts on the kettle to boil for the Nescafé and prepares a solution of bleach and soapy water for the rug.

When she gets back to the dining room no one is there, but the dog, Lucrezia, has mounted the table and is trampling the remains of dinner into the cloth with her paws and splattering sauce from dishes with her great purple tongue. She pushes the animal hopefully but it digs in and she can hear the sound of its claws gouging the surface of the wood. She opens the folding doors and peers cautiously into the lounge. The room is empty. She takes in her bowl of soapy water and begins dabbing at the stain on the rug. She works quickly and has made the mark fade considerably by the time they all burst back in to tell her they have been putting Lionel to bed.

Roxanne wants to dance. 'The rug?' Mirabel whimpers but Roxanne says for Christ's sake, life is for living. She whips the tainted rug from the floor and rolls it up in a corner. Benjamin puts on a rock record and Roxanne begins to gyrate, digging her workman's boots into the polished parquet floor.

Mirabel takes her mind off it by thinking about the neighbours. She imagines she hears a thumping on the wall but cannot make up her mind if it is the music, which is very loud, or Mrs Winter with a shoe, urging its cessation. In her mind she paraphrases the events of the evening for serving up to her neighbours the following day, along with the remains of the kidneys, browned under the grill with crumbs and freshened up with some lettuce leaves, but these thoughts have to be discarded. Her neighbours do not take kindly to noise and are unlikely to be on speaking terms with her for a time.

Dancing, Roxanne exists in a different plane. Her face is washed clean of all its charlady's conflicts and deprivations, her lumpish limbs take flight. She has shaken off her combat jacket and her large breasts pummel wantonly at a greying tee shirt. Mirabel finds her eyes drawn to this swift-moving, sensual Roxanne. Benjamin too is mesmerized. His eyes are glazed. He positively drools. When Sybil whines that she wants a piece of the action, he rises like a sleepwalker and falls gratefully into her tense clutches.

Roxanne's hands slice the air like a solitary juggler. Benjamin struggles round the floor with Sybil like a wrestler on the final round but his smile is full of happiness and his palms are filled with her buttocks. When she moves away, snakelike, to change the record, Benjamin collapses into a chair in ecstatic languor. Mirabel takes advantage of his state and sits on his knee and puts her tongue in his mouth, but he pushes her off and tells her not to make an exhibition of herself. She looks around for someone to talk to. Lionel is still in bed and there is only Norma, sitting in her fur coat on the clean end of the sofa, and the dog, trailing dinner all over the floor on its paws. She would like to have a word with Flora to find out what the future holds but Flora seems to have disappeared. 'Where's Flora?' she says to no one in particular. Sybil stops dancing abruptly. She stamps across the room and switches off the music. 'Flora!' she calls out harshly. She glares around the room, then at each of the guests in turn as if they might have hidden the diminutive Flora in a pocket or handbag. 'What's going on?' says Mirabel mildly. Sybil's face has taken on a peculiar, beaky, frozen aspect, like a hen immortalized in stone.

Norma's face, on the other hand, is of a particularly vivid pink from the effort of trying to suppress some giant mirth which escapes in small squeaks and snorts. At length there comes a soft chortle, increasing in volume, on and on, chortle, chortle, chortle, chortle, whee, whee, so that one expects to see a train emerging from the tunnel of her mouth. 'What is it?' Mirabel says in horror. Norma raises distraught eyes at the ceiling. 'She must be a rattler in the sack,' she howls.

Sybil's green eyes narrow. Her lips compress into purple wafers. 'I hardly think you're in a position to pass comments,' she hisses. '*Anyone* who would wear a mink coat to Neasden . . .'

Norma's jaw falls. Her look is helpless in the face of Sybil's marksmanship. Two huge tears shiver in her eyelids and then plop into her blue fur. She looks to each of them in turn, beseechingly, reproachfully. None of them is able to speak. Now that the music and the loud debate have been killed they are compelled to strain their ears to the faint gibbering of springs above their heads.

Without a word she grabs her handbag and marches from the room, slamming two doors so viciously that a little china bird falls from the wall and explodes upon the wooden floor.

'She was giving me a lift home,' Roxanne says after a time. 'How am I supposed to get home?' 'I shall take you,' Sybil offers. She claims her dog and her overcoat, and eventually, Mirabel's lifeless hand. 'It's been so pleasant,' she says. The two women make a perfectly normal exit, dragging the dog.

'Well, my girl,' says Benjamin when Sybil's little sporty number has ripped through the exterior silence. 'You have to admit I know some interesting types.' 'They're in our bed,' Mirabel says. 'Together.' 'For God's sake,' Benjamin savagely slaps her bottom. 'Men and women do that sort of thing' – he guffaws – 'Don't tell me I married a prude.' A rapid chorus of strange, tormented sighs, quite loud, drifts from the bedroom. Mirabel thinks of the holy souls in purgatory. Benjamin's face twitches in embarrassment.

'None of this would have happened,' he accuses, 'if you'd had the good grace to offer a drop of hot coffee.' His face lights up quite unexpectedly. 'Coffee! That's it!' He strides to the stairs and arranges his expression into one of benign joviality. 'Coffee's ready,' he bellows up the steps. He swivels around to his wife, eyes full of cunning. 'That'll flush them out,' he predicts.

The four of them sit around the lounge drinking re-boiled instant. Flora is neat and calm as ever but Lionel unzipped, unbuttoned, unshaven, looks completely beyond repair. Mirabel still wants to ask Flora to tell her fortune even though she is no longer sure she can trust her future to a woman who seeks her satisfactions so unpremeditatedly. 'I'd like you to make a prediction,' she says quickly and nervously, stirring at the thick liquid in her cup. 'Sorry?' Flora says cheerfully. 'You know, tell my stars,' says Mirabel. Flora stares at her hard for a moment before rudely addressing herself to Benjamin. 'What's she on about?'

'Search me,' Benjamin sniggers.

'I'm sorry,' Mirabel says. 'I ought not to have pursued it but it's the first time I've met a seer and I thought it would be ever so interesting...' She trails off. Flora squints in honest bewilderment. 'Blimey dear,' says the priestess. 'Your ears need washing. I'm not a seer, I'm an overseer. At the factory. Overlocking department.'

'Benjamin,' Mirabel pleads.

'It ought to have been Mrs Arnott from Pressing,' Benjamin reasons. 'She's a gifted amateur comedienne. She keeps us all in stitches. Alas, she received offer of a paid engagement.'

A small nerve begins to vibrate in Mirabel's jaw. At last she cries out: 'Who are all these people? I don't know them. You don't know them. We'll never see them again. We never do.' She begins to gather up cups and saucers, heedless of the breakage potential in her trembling fingers. Tears stand out in her eyes.

Benjamin strikes his knee so hard that his own cup of coffee leaps out of his hand and into the sofa. 'Good God, girl,' he says. 'Where is your sense of spontaneity?' Mirabel shakes her head in guilt and perplexity. She does not know. She has been cooking all week for the party. She goes to the kitchen and stays there, running scalding water over her hands to improve their circulation, until she hears Benjamin bundling the last of the guests into the back seat of his car.

When he gets home the dishes have been washed, the sheets on the bed have been changed and Mirabel has swept and mopped the floor. The house, no longer disastrous, wears a rakish expression. Benjamin waltzes about, humming fragments of a tune played earlier on the record machine. 'Wonderful meal, darling,' he reminisces. Mirabel is on her knees, scrubbing vigorously at the rug.

'I say, rather a Bohemian lot,' he establishes. When she has finished with the rug, she will go to work on the sofa. 'God, those women dancing!' He does a thing with his fist to signify sexual arousal. Mirabel grunts with concentration. It is a challenge to her, this carnival of disrupted substances which must be cast out before they have had time to claim tenure. She does not care if it takes all night. Benjamin bends down to plant a kiss on top of her pneumatic head which moves in time with her urgent fists. He notes that on her pale, tired face, a tiny smile is starting and he is gratified to have married a woman who appreciates the good things in life. 'Jolly good evening, actually, dear,' he says fondly.

Mirabel does not hear. As her fingers travel through matted trails of animal hair, her mind charges to a primitive hunting call. She will be up early in the morning to wash out the tablecloth, remove the mud from the carpet in the hall. In the back of her head, there is a foetal thought which shifts and grows and claims its space so assertively as to blot out everything else, even the dancing figure of her husband.

She half hopes the sofa is beyond repair.

There advances on her ear the distant shrill and stampede of the sales; the remnant counter, rich in colour and danger as an Eastern bazaar. Her blood is up, she can feel it. It is almost time she went scouring the sales for newer material for fresher covers. Her hands, already in imagination plundering bales and billows of cloth costing good money, are guiltless. She has to keep the place nice in case of visitors.

Black Ice

Violet Jones went on a skiing holiday and she never came back. It is a dream that many girls order for their hearts, recklessly forsaking heated offices, strapping themselves on to planks and sliding off into the costly cold in dread of their lives. Violet's friends, Jane and Marjorie, still talk about her. She was out of the ordinary, they have to admit. Though who'd have thought it?

In a way Violet's friends pushed her around as much as Stephen did. She didn't mind Stephen treating her badly. She was lucky to have him. His occasional attentions singled her out and made her special. Most of the time she suffered terribly but stubbornly because she preferred having her bones turned to water now and again when he was nice to her than to calcify with one of her own kind, grey on grey, safe and useful like stones in a wall.

Stephen travelled a lot. His departures were sudden; the crump of his American leather flee bag in the back of the car, the gasp of tyre rubber and he was torn away from her to some part of the world for an unspecified period. He was successful, which meant that business and pleasure merged in his travels like vinegar and butter in a sauce. He never wrote to her when he was away, although it might be weeks, and when he came back he seemed utterly fulfilled. Sometimes she wondered why he bothered with her. There were, in truth, quite long stretches of his homebound time when he did not. But he always returned to her.

'You must leave him,' Marjorie said when she found her alone and in a mess. 'It's clear he doesn't love you.'

'Of course he loves me.' Violet was offended. 'It's his life. He has to travel.'

'Why doesn't he take you with him?' Joan demanded.

'I never asked him,' Violet pleaded.

'Well then, ask,' Joan snapped.

'That's right,' Marjorie added. 'It's time you gave him a piece of your mind.'

A piece of her mind. She could see it like a little sample slice of wedding cake, snug inside paper lace and silver box. She had no idea how to apportion herself. She had given him everything, allowed herself to be consumed. All the same, she told herself to shut out their voices, I belong to him. I am a label, stitched inside his clothing. As soon as she said it, she was haunted by this image of herself, faded and forgotten, locked away out of the limelight.

'I have to go away,' Stephen said on a night when he had made love to her, meticulous and absent-minded as a woman darning a sock.

'Take me with you?' She gave him a piece of Marjorie's mind.

He opened his eyes to watch her. 'All right. If that's what you want.'

She did not wish to pry but after a time she thought she must ask him where they were going.

'To the highest mountains.'

'Oh,' she said.

'Skiing.'

'Oh – oh,' she said.

It was night time when they arrived at an alpine peak and settled into a hotel that was a little gingerbread house haphazardly iced with snow. 'Look!' she said, throwing open the windows in their toasty room to allow the cold air to ruffle the frill of her negligée across her bosom, to show him the lacy white outline of mountains right outside their window. She felt mad with happiness, having got him all to herself in this godforsaken place, even though it was hard to claim his attention.

'Look, darling!' The icy air at least must disturb him.

Stephen's brown limbs were disposed on the eiderdown. He was reading some sort of map. He looked up dreamily, murmuring about runs, blue and red and black, and then she thought he must be a bit tiddly because he said something that sounded like 'horse pissed'.

She came to him and he claimed her vigorously and vacantly, as though limbering up for the more important sport. Just before they went to sleep he said: 'What's your level?' She cast around wildly in her brain for a mature answer for he seemed to be very serious. 'How much skiing have you done?' he pursued with a sigh. 'None,' she mumbled into his shoulder. 'Damn it, you are a goose,' he said. 'I'll have to find you an instructor. You'll have to get fitted up for skis.' She stroked his back to calm him down. She wanted to sleep, to fashion her dreams to his lovely shape. 'In the morning,' she said, 'we'll have a long, lazy breakfast in bed and then we'll plan.'

He tore himself away from her. 'What sort of holiday do you think this is anyway?' He moved to the cold side of the bed to emphasize its spartan prospect. She plucked at the pillow and wept on it for half an hour and then she fell asleep, dreaming of runs, blue and red and black. These did not feature on an alpine slope but in the stockings of a line of ill-looking chorus girls – herself among them – who danced out of step.

When she awoke, he was already gone. She looked to see if he had left a note but he had not. She picked up the telephone. 'Déjeuner?' she whispered into it hopefully, adding her room number, and was surprised when it came almost immediately, bubbling and delicious, brought by a little dark girl who was pretty and friendly. The maid settled the breakfast on the table. She pulled the curtains and then stood back and smiled at Violet with modest pride. Violet wandered to the window, sipping her coffee, and looked at the two huge mountains that swept up before her, only a snowball's throw from where she stood.

She nodded at the maid who was conscious of her duty to show them off, and then gave her attention back to the view. In the streets, she noted, everyone carried skis on their shoulders, with the casual pride of black women in Africa who carry babies on their hips.

After breakfast she went out and walked to the bottom slopes where she sat at an outdoor café. She saw now that the two mountains did not really spring up beneath her bedroom window. In fact the whole village nestled between them and was held up to the sky on their giant wings as if balanced on the back of an eagle. It was the strangest place she had ever been in. Big-footed butterflies circled the air and a line of chocolate-coloured coons came gliding past her like the chorus of a minstrel show. She couldn't ask. Everyone else seemed to take it for granted. It was ages before she came to recognize the queer lepidoptera as hang gliders on skis and realized that the sun-wizened champions of the slopes, their skin tough and brown as shoe leather, still bothered to protect their lips with an opaque white slice of barrier cream.

The mountains had been claimed for a giant playground. From a distance the skiers were like jelly beans in their bright padded clothing. Some zig-zagged across little slopes, some wriggled down the sides of mountains. There were even those who alleviated the boredom with the possibility of death, jumping from one slope to another and executing a somersault in between. The only ones who looked responsible were the children. Tiny infants in padded suits (they might have been pram suits) flew past, their pink faces hardened by concentration. So small, so much in command of their expanse of pristine white, they reminded her of Santas on a Christmas cake.

Quite high she saw a man skiing boastfully and strung out behind him, like the trail of a kite, a line of women on skis. 'It must be Stephen,' she thought but then she saw that it was a boy, much younger than Stephen and that his hair was cut like a toilet brush.

'Look up, pleeze.' There was a flash and she turned around disconcerted. 'Smile pleeze.' The photographer used another exposure.

His face was so handsome that she could not help staring while the little flashes exhausted themselves like flies on a candle. There was something wrong with his handsome smile. It was twisted with the contempt of the professional ingrate. She looked away quickly, as if she had been caught gaping at a birth mark. 'You are a nice girl,' he wheedled. 'Look up, pleeze.'

She was rescued by Stephen. He came up behind her and took the card the photographer held out. 'Oh,' she yelped in relief. 'Where have you been?' 'At the next café. Come and join us.' Us. Her heart iced over. She shook little coins out on the table and followed him to a table at the café where three wonderful girls dipped wet red lips into cups of chocolate.

That day Stephen was quite kind to her. He took her to the ski shop and supervised the hiring of her equipment. He booked her tuition and insisted on waiting with her for the arrival of the instructor he had chosen.

Half a dozen other beginners were waiting, a couple welded by their new marriage, some young and unattached people who viewed one another and Violet with the same rejecting looks she gave to them, recognizing each other's ordinariness and incapacity to wrestle fate; a middle-aged couple, helium filled, bouncing and barking.

When the instructor arrived Violet recognized his haircut. It was the boy who had led a tail of girls on the slopes. She thought now that she had imagined eagerness in their pursuit.

Close up he was not attractive. His face was sharp, the shrewd face of a peasant. The ends of his mouth turned down. He greeted Stephen with an embrace and the formal handshake common to the area. Violet he met with a curt nod used for inferiors. He counted the class with his eyes as if counting money and wrote down their names. His name, he said, was Jim.

'Follow me.' He led them to a nursery slope. Stephen came with them, solicitously carrying her skis. The boy turned with a contemptuous nod. 'She can carry her own skis. She needs the exercise.'

Stephen allowed the crippling bundle to collapse on her shoulders and she tottered off after the other burdened holidaymakers, after the agile youth whose name was gym.

The boy walked like a shepherd. His body was angled to peaks and slopes. He belonged to the mountains. When they reached the lift and had put on their skis he attached them each to a hanging metal pole on a pulley and they were dragged up the side of the mountain, rigid, with fear, as electric hares.

'One by one,' he commanded when they had reached the top. 'I wait here.' He pointed his ski pole at a middle-aged woman who went slithering off, grim and shapeless like a ghost in the night. 'You!' he ordered Violet. She scrabbled forward with her poles like a cripple at a holy shrine, intent on a miracle. There was a sickening slide and she landed, quite pleasantly, on her bottom. 'Lean forward, bend your knees,' the boy shouted, harsh and dictatorial.

She poked a pole in the snow and pulled herself to her feet. Her mouth was set. She propelled herself as if rowing a canoe. She fell again, but faster. 'Hey, you!' the boy shouted down. 'You should donate your knees to medical science.'

'My name,' she called back, aggrieved, 'is Violet.'

He skiied down to where she was and watched her with amusement. 'Violette,' he said very softly. He put out a hand and pulled her to her feet.

The following day she was up quite eagerly, hauling her skis to the slopes, clamping them to her agonized feet. She thought, while she waited, of the bleeding toes of ballerinas, of joggers' nipples. Everyone suffered in the interest of self-improvement. She had never been prepared to acquaint herself with pain. She allowed it to lie in wait. 'Here he is!' The plump young honeymooner with bright blonde hair disturbed her thoughts. Her voice was bitter. 'He's all right, really,' said the middle-aged woman whose name was Barbara. 'You've got to give as good as you get.'

She looked down at the slight figure stamping up the hill towards them. His goat's eyes glittered as indifferently as rocks of chrysolite. There was a mutinous bristling among the learners as he advanced but when he arrived he imposed his assurance on them and they only wanted to stay close to him.

'Weight on your downhill ski, lean outward. Come on, Baa-baa-raa!' When he called out to the hopeless middle-aged skier, he made his voice low and rough so that her name became the bleating of a sheep. Her legs parted unwillingly as she forced herself to a snow plough stop. 'Show some respect,' she begged. 'I am old enough to be your mother.' He laughed. 'I would not teach my mother to ski.' The blonde who had just got married and was cocooned in her husband's worship was brave enough to speak out. 'Well, you're getting paid to teach us,' she said. The boy's eyes shone with amusement. He did an exultant twirling leap in mid air and landed perfectly on his skis. 'So I teach you,' he said. 'Come on, Miss Piggy.' Her yellow curls and her round bust shook with fury. 'My name,' she said, 'is Deborah.' He looked bewildered. 'No,' he said. 'To me you are Miss Piggy. She is very beautiful – and you also. I think I am a little in love.' Violet laughed unwisely. He caught her eye. 'Now,' he said, 'Violette will show how it is properly done. Violette.' He repeated her name softly for his own enjoyment. She moved off in a traverse.

As she executed a turn which he had demonstrated, she slid down in a sickening tangle of legs. One of her skis came off and she had to scramble down to retrieve it. She waited for the kind hand to pull her to her feet but there was nothing, only her own undignified gasps of fear and the hateful mocking voice, from the top of the slope, of the youth. 'Violette is the acrobat. She skis backward. Violette says it is better to fall gently than to ski well.'

He showed them a terrible thing. He herded them to a higher peak where they had to slide all the way down in order to attain momentum to ascend the opposite slope. It was called *schussing*; skis pointing down, no control. One could travel at sixty miles an hour, he mused. One by one the petrified learners shot down like lemmings. Only Violet clung to the top of the slope with edged skis. 'No,' she said. She tried to make her voice firm. He touched her with his oddly delicate touch and smiled. 'Go, Violette. It is not possible to fall. Go, or I push you.' His touch became pressure. 'No!' She had to cling on to his arm to stop herself from falling. 'I am terrified.' 'Terrified,' he sang out in mocking fashion. 'How you say it. You have never known terror in your life. All of life is on the edge of the mountain. Terror and joy. There is no life unless you let go. Go, Violette.' He pushed hard. She let out a little shriek as she began to slide. It was an extraordinary moment. It was the moment of death, the realization in an instant, that there was no going back, nothing but fate. After the initial shock, she began to sense the freedom of fatality. She was a car with no brakes (no car either) – an element in the grip of an element. She skimmed the snow like a mayfly on water. She felt astonishingly light. She was gaining momentum. She skudded over hard icy lumps. She was going faster.

She began to be afraid, thinking of sixty miles an hour, thinking she must go faster and faster until hurtled into some immovable substance that would smash her up like a snowball. She saw the pieces of herself flying in different directions, brightly coloured, irresponsible as balloons. Absurd, she thought, to fear such an end. This was life and the other thing was death. Even here there was an alternative. It was simply that one did not have to make the choice.

She could not see ahead. There was a series of small bumps and she had to approach them blindly, seeing nothing but bump and sky and far-off snow peaks. If she had the tiniest wings she would be flying. If she had a bigger slope – a precipice – she would be flying. 'Oh, please,' she prayed suddenly, 'let me live at least today so that I can tell Stephen how happy I've been. After that, I won't care.'

Her foot caught on some frozen lump and went flying away from her. She tried to get it back but her other leg was now pursuing a different course. 'Oh, well,' she thought. 'This is it.'

She sprawled and went flying along the snow. She could feel its surface merging with her skin, piling under her sunglasses, into her eyes and mouth. Every bit of her was furred with snow. The more powerful element was claiming her.

The mountain, suddenly, stopped whizzing. She lay perfectly still. Her hand moved. She brought it up slowly and attempted to remove some snow from her face with a mitten but it too was snow packed. She lay uncaring for a long time before she looked up. Ahead of her, more bumps and the clear profile of the ascending slope. These were just the baby slopes. Proficient skiers went down sheer mountain faces, negotiating hills of solid ice which were called moguls. She had barely acquainted herself with terror. The whole spectrum lay ahead. Scraping herself to her feet, she was shaken by weary laughter, like a fit of coughing. Too tired to edge her skis, she began immediately to slide into an ungainly *schuss*. Speed took her like a lover and she laughed with it, as lovers are supposed to do behind locked doors, the rest of the way down and all the way back up.

The boy was waiting for her. Slowed by gravity she had a chance to study him, the smooth line of his jaw, his contemptuous eye. 'It's only a contempt of artifice,' she thought. 'He's young. He still believes in life.' She thought there was a new look to his expression. 'Violette,' he said. Emotion gave his voice a swooning quality and a part of her rushed to meet it. 'I'm all right,' she said softly. He shook his head sadly. 'No.' He made one of his surprising leaps and turned to face her, impish under toilet-brush hair. 'You are as supple as a bag of potatoes.'

The air, the sun, the vigorous exercise were working on her. Her exhilaration would not fade. Her skin glowed. She could not find Stephen in the place appointed for lunch so she went instead to the shops and bought some flimsy resort clothes from one of the boutiques. She put on her new outfit and went to wait for Stephen in the bar of the hotel. She drank cocktails and made small talk with everyone who came and went, whatever their sex, generous in the knowledge that of all of them, she was the one who was waiting for Stephen.

She had had eight drinks and visited the lavatory once to be sick by the time he came in. It was ten o'clock. Little flurries of snow caught around his collar. He shook himself like a dog and sat down looking radiant. In spite of her efforts, he was much too good for her.

'Where were you?' she said bleakly.

'Skiing.' He angled his eyebrows and picked up a menu from the bar.

'The lifts close at five o'clock.'

He shrugged indifferently and called for whisky. 'Time flies when you're having fun,' he said.

'It goes slowly when you're on your own and out of your depth and in love,' she said. 'I know you can have every girl on the mountain. I know. You don't have to prove it to me.' He put down the menu. He looked at her. She thought he would hit her on the jaw. He sighed. How just he looked, how wronged. 'Please don't say these things,' he reasoned. 'You are making me very unhappy.'

That night the snow came. She was woken by the shutters banging and the whoosh of wind. She went to close the shutters and was bewildered for a moment when she could not see the hard jaws of the mountains but only fluffy inconsequential stuff like sugar thrown at the windows. 'I'm glad,' she thought, picturing the skiers planted like disappointed jelly beans in the bowl of the blizzard, thinking of her lover who would be forced to stay with her in bed.

She woke to the sound of the wind howling, to solitude. 'He can't,' she thought. She ran to the window and looked out. A swarm of snowflakes attacked the panes.

'It is a terrible morning,' she told the maid when her breakfast was brought.

'Oui.'

'No skiing today.'

'Mais oui!' The maid indicated with an eye the space that had been vacated by Stephen. She sucked on her words to make them English. 'All pretty ladies, they too go. He is liking to teach them. Him they follow all the days, all the weathers. He is not eager to get away.'

The woman's hateful little black eyes were lit dully like olive stones. Rage and hopelessness battled in Violet's breast. He would teach other girls to ski, having handed her to the callous youth. Tears crammed her eyes but she would not make a fool of herself in front of the maid. 'Please don't say these things,' she insisted with dignity. 'You are making me very unhappy.' The woman watched her for a moment and then, surprisingly, she flung out a wild laugh. 'I cannot make you unhappy. I cannot make you happy. I only make the bed.'

Violet went out after breakfast. She put on all the clothes she could find but the snow still found her face and made her a corrosive mask. She felt like Doctor Zhivago, walking off into the storm, bereft of all that was loved. At the same time she felt lightheaded, curiously free. She did not wonder what Jane and Marjorie would think of what she was about to do. She scarcely considered Stephen.

She took a lift to the blasted place where she had made acquaintance with terror. When she came out of the cable car with a few grimly experienced skiers she found that the view had vanished, that peaks and bumps and moguls had been shrouded in a ragged white veil. She stood at the top of the slope, holding her breath, not moving for as long as she could and then slowly she allowed her skis to slip around until the earth slid back beneath her feet. She leaned forward and closed her eyes. In a minute she was whirling through space, timeless, weightless. At first, as she gained speed she could feel the pain of tiny icy snowflakes smashing on her face and then her skin went numb and there was no feeling except motion, no sound but the racing wind. Down, down she flew, skidding and sliding and gliding and flying. Up she went, rising like the mountain towards the sky. If she kept her eyes closed she knew she would not fall, she thought she might keep going until the mountain ran out and she was sailing through the air. In fact she continued, upright and upward until gravity seized her and slowed her and brought her back to earth.

She opened her eyes and saw to her relief that she had stopped on course, only ten yards or so from the lift. Even the hardiest skiers had abandoned the mountain. There was just a single figure, his bare head thistled with ice, snow swirling around him. 'He's made of stone,' she thought.

'So,' the boy said. 'Nothing broken?'

She undid her skis and walked up to him. 'My heart,' she said. He studied her. 'I believe you. *Pas grave.*' He went with her to the lift. 'Violette,' he said. 'I am going to buy you a drink.' She frowned in her surprise. 'I have to look for my friend.' 'Ah, yes,' he smiled. 'Your friend. There is no need to look. He is at *l'Escargot.*'

'Thank you,' she said.

He shrugged indifferently.

'You can come too, if you like.'

'Perhaps.' Already, she thought, his mind was elsewhere.

Half an hour later she went into the *Escargot*. There were long wooden tables in the bar, full of red-faced skiers drinking *vin chaud*, a drink the colour of boot polish with bits of fruit floating unsuccessfully on top. The young men and women were all Stephen's kind, accomplished skiers, properly dressed and perfectly tanned. They seemed wonderfully amused by their own talk. They were drinking unwisely and over the tans their faces were red as radishes. They seemed fused together so that she could not immediately identify Stephen from the other successful young men. She saw only one face that she knew. The boy sat aloof and composed as an owl, his eyes cold and watchful. He was drinking hot chocolate. Occasionally he was snared in the rattle of communal mirth and his cynical mouth would twitch into a loose, foolish young grin. His eyes did not flicker except once, to catch her in their baleful glare. They were the palest green she had ever seen, green like thinly sliced kiwi fruit. He had no pupils. She had only once seen eyes like that before when she was a child and her favourite cat, exposed in direct sunlight, showed jaws gripped around a squirming mouse and his teddy-bear button eyes showed palest, alien green. 'What can he want?' she wondered. For an instant something human moved in his glance and his eyes locked into hers like a lover, comfortable and conspiratorial. 'He knows me,' she thought and was amazed. 'We're two of a kind. We want the same thing.'

'I have fallen for my ski instructor,' she wrote on a postcard to her girlfriends. She did not send it. There was nothing she could say to make them approve. On the slopes he remained distant. She was learning to ski, slowly, lumpishly. She still fell a lot and it was then they engaged in their only intimacy, when he helped her to her feet, murmuring her name, Violette.

He never assisted the other skiers. They were left flailing and furious in the snow. In spite of this they were all, men and women attracted to him. Women had a way of looking at him. They put their asses out on their eyes. Men offered to buy him drinks. They stuffed the pockets of his tee shirts with cigars. She thought of the other boy whose name was Jim, whose friends were very fond of him. He made no effort to appeal. He was what he was.

She no longer knew which of them was following the other, how they met, without appointment in some café each day. She was confused by him, suffused. Everything else seemed as unreal as the butterflies which were hang gliders. Her mind was filled with pale green eyes, a thin mouth that held her name like a flower.

'Have you ever broken any bones?' she asked him one day. She wanted to sculpt him to a fit for her heart. She wanted to feel tenderness.

'Yes.' He stretched in a manner that proved the shattered tissue usefully remade. 'You,' he reprimanded, 'have never broken a bone. Not one little finger. It is very important for you to make good bones for the worms.'

She felt her bones imprisoned inside cowardly flesh. At the same time she sensed their independence, their relationship to nerve and muscle, their function of service and power. She was changing. He was evolving her. She did not imagine it. Stephen noticed, too. He no longer neglected her. He had started meeting her after her lesson. He accompanied them when they went for drinks. Bronzed and tautened, released from self-pity, she did not hamper him. They looked like any other handsome couple at the resort. It was a pity that she no longer loved him.

In response to the boy she reached out her little finger. He could break it if he wanted. She did not care. So far, he had scarcely touched her, except to help her to her feet. Sometimes in the snow, he brushed past her like a cat and when she met his look it was insolent. At first it unnerved her. She was ready for him now. He did not accept her finger. He said slowly, 'Yes, I think you know. I live quite close to here. I have an apartment. I would like you to come back with me.' 'My friend ...' she said to draw him into a conspiracy to get rid of Stephen. He nodded formally. 'Of course. Your friend is invited too.'

The wind had died. They walked together in a light, woolly fall of snow to the place where he lived. She had got over her disappointment at having to invite Stephen. Jim stamped along with his soldier's walk. He would know what to do about Stephen. One could tell he was a seasoned campaigner. It was important to her to see the place where he lived. Now that he had laid claim to her, she felt sure he would not let her go. She felt at ease in the grip of his will. Out here in the mountains she would grow fearless and free (free of Jane and Marjorie), although she crossed her fingers when she said 'free'. Already, at the back of her mind, she pictured a more tender alliance, a time in the future when she would grow into him as frail, tender flowers grow into the bare face of the mountain.

Jim lived in a single room with a big black bed and walls adorned with posters of brutal pop stars. Tiny sections were boarded off for kitchen and bathroom. He was proud of his territory. She went to pains to admire it and felt cross at Stephen for the careless way in which he flung himself on the bed and said he needed a drink.

'There is only coffee,' Jim said, resentful at the failure of his hospitality.

'That will be fine,' Violet said.

'Don't you drink?' Stephen said.

'I only drink very good wine,' he said stiffly. Violet could see that he was offended. She had not seen him so disturbed before. It gave her an advantage. She wanted to be alone with him so that she could make it up to him.

'It's all right,' she soothed.

'What is this very good wine?' Stephen provoked. 'Tell us and we will get some.'

The boy named an uncommon wine of the region which she had once tasted, not very good. 'It is difficult to purchase.' He named a shop at the beginning of the next village, almost a mile away. 'Only at this shop is it sold.'

Violet could not contain a little smile of admiration. It was a plan to get rid of Stephen. 'If it is too much trouble ...' Jim said to him courteously. Stephen laughed. 'It's no trouble.' Nothing was too much trouble if it was for Jim. Everyone felt the same way. Stephen rose from the bed and put a familiar arm around Violet. 'She will go. She needs the exercise.' She heard the boy laughing in polite collusion as she left the room and went quickly into the street.

She began walking in the direction of the next village. She was not resentful, not really. She trusted Jim, accepted his leadership. Her brain was not quick. It was not for her to anticipate, merely to accept the truths he offered her and turn them, on her own account, into courage. It occurred to her that he might use the time to tell Stephen that she now belonged to him. All the same, she thought, she was not acting very bravely running away, leaving him to do the dirty work. Perhaps he's testing me, she then thought forlornly, and was stuck to the glittering pavement in panic, rooting in her brain, this cell and that, for a key to the puzzle. She turned into the nearest *épicerie* and heedlessly purchased a bottle of Muscadet. She ran all the way back to the apartment block and then paused to catch her foolish breath before opening the door slowly, silently – just a crack – like a child in a game of suspense.

Jim was in bed. She stood spying in the minute gap of the door, on his smooth torso beneath the black cover, his green eyes focussed blankly on the ceiling. He had got rid of Stephen. He was waiting for her. She heard his little gasp of delighted surprise as she whirled through the door and turned, laughing, with her back against it, to face him. The green eyes gazed at her with their usual mixture of amusement and contempt, giving no clue to the feelings that worked behind them. Stephen's brown eyes watched her with their old look of exasperation from the pillow just an inch, Christ, half an inch, from the line of vision she had allowed herself in the opening of the door. Only once, for a moment, was there any change to this view when the boy's pale eyes melted with a look of uncharacteristic tenderness, when a hand moved beneath the blanket and he gave another gasp of delighted surprise.

The waiter hissed and grumbled when he brought her her drink. Crazy damn foreigner, to sit outside in a blizzard. She would not go into the café. Even from here she could hear laughter. Out of doors it was cold and clean.

There was a little line of glasses on the table in front of her. She would not let the waiter take them. She told him she wanted to keep count. She latched her teeth on to the rim of the glass and gulped back the hot wine. Sooner or later she would be all right.

There was a flash of light. 'Look up, pleeze?'

Violet recognized the tone of eager despair and growled in exasperation. 'Go away.' She did not care what impression she made. 'Leave me alone.'

'One moment, pleeze. Take off your glasses, look at me pleeze. You are a very nice girl.' The photographer danced around her like a kicked dog.

She took off her dark glasses slowly and lifted to him the red ruin of her weeping face. He offered her his wheedling smile; 'Do you mind?' Already he was seating himself. She raised an eyebrow to query his presumptuousness but the waiter, seeing another customer, had come out and 'Whisky,' the photographer quickly answered her questioning frown.

There was a moment, after she had paid for his drink when

she noticed that his smile had lost its subordinate look. He watched her so boldly that she made mental count of the money in her purse, knowing that a contest of drinking was to follow and that she would be expected to pay. 'What can he want?' she wondered miserably, trapped in his gaze; and then she understood and smiled with relief for she knew she was not always very bright. 'He knows me,' she accepted. 'We're two of a kind.'

For Your Own Bad

'Have you ever been in love?' Dora shuffled up in her dreadful purple dressing-gown and her furry slippers, her box clutched in her right hand and caressed by the fingers of her left, and pushed her little grey face into mine.

'Yes.' She didn't really want to know. We were not friends. We were patients, which is a virtue, so we smiled at each other as we made paper roses or nodded from behind our cocoa.

'Tell us about it.' The nervous fingers of her left hand pried and prised at the box, threatening to open it and we both looked away in horror. What was in the box was a secret, she had told us proudly. To me it seemed that if Dora's box was opened the troubles of the world would fly out. I knew mad people. I was mad myself. My heart could not contain the sadness of seeing the lid lifted and the broken crayons, the sweet papers, the holy pictures inside.

Once I fell in love with a bouquet of sheep. They hung together on the side of a hill, eyeing me with their shy, sly, innocent faces and then ran away all in a bunch like school-girls, with skinny legs in snow-white socks.

'Baa-a-ah!' I echoed. One sheep stopped and swivelled around, grinning, its yellow eyes marvellously mad.

Once I fell in love with a carving knife. I wanted to give it soft, pastel places to play so I cut my lover's throat.

'Why did you do it?'

'Because I am mad, my Lord.'

'But not so mad as to be unaware that insanity is a plea for mitigation within the law.'

'No, my Lord – not that mad.'

If you are mad they put you away for your own good. If you are sane they put you away for your own bad. They took away my knife and put me away for my own good.

Once I fell in love with a man. I met him in bed one morning in Majorca. Sitting up, fighting off the awful heat; my mouth, my eyes and my mind shut up and dank, like little shops in the off season, I came across a person in the bed.

He was naked, as much as I could see, and smiling. 'Was it wonderful for you last night, my darling?' he said through a gleaming, melon-slice grin.

'What?'

He laughed, a devil's laugh, a small boy's laugh.

'Did we ... ?' To be thirty and know so little. Could it happen without a person even knowing it? He laughed again, kicking the sheets up in his delight. No clothes on at all. 'Not yet, little flower.'

With relief, I found the strength for irritation. 'How did you get into my apartment? How did you get into my bed?' I pushed back my hair and pulled the sheets about myself.

'I drove you here, carried you here, put you to bed and then realized that, like you, I was too drunk for anything but sleep.'

I felt myself thawing in the heat of embarrassment. So this is what it was like to wake up in bed in the morning with a man. He was a wonderful-looking creature, all black curls and brown skin, a bit younger than me, and English, though he looked foreign.

My dreaming stare drew him close and his hand crept under my piece of sheet. So this is what it was like. 'I can't.' I told him. 'I've made myself a promise that the only man I'll sleep with is the man I marry. I've waited so long.'

The demon laughed again and his hand, so gentle and warm, moved in a way too tender to be outrageous. 'You know you've already slept with a man,' he said. 'You are waiting to make love with the man you will marry.'

His face moved close and every bit of it was good to look at. 'Perhaps,' he said, 'you have already met him.'

We did it and it wasn't too bad. I watched his body moving in happy anguish and knew that nobody would mind if I touched his curls. I am falling in love, I thought, while he smiled and sighed and mumbled his delight in me.

Love is so pleasant, I thought. It takes so little cleverness and so few people and it takes up so much time. Without love, I thought, I would already be striding along the shore in anger with my book and my Lilo, searching in vain for shade and body space – and love.

There was one awkward moment later when we were drinking coffee and he said he had to be going.

'Going?'

He flashed his grin and waved his hands in an apology and the dismissal of an apology. 'Before I met you I had a life of my own. There are still bits of it here and there.' He was dressed in white pants and a blue shirt and was knotting the sleeves of a navy sweater around his neck. 'I'll be back,' he said.

He kissed me and walked away and out the door, then back – a laughing head. 'By the way, I don't know your name.'

'Mildred.' The door slammed and he was gone. I didn't know if he had heard.

Mildred is what I said. What else? Still, my name is not without significance. It tells that my mother was a woman of no imagination but great determination. Her mother was Mildred, she was Mildred, so what on earth else should I be? As for poor old pa, he might have mentioned names like Jennifer and Rose, but if he did, no one heard.

What I remember most about my mother is laughter. She was fat and she laughed all the time. She laughed at us and for us because poor old pa and me didn't laugh much at all, didn't see much to laugh at.

Her nerve endings were buried deep in the fat, you see – not exposed to the tripwires of tension and terror. Pa and I, a man without power and a girl without prettiness, used to put down our knives and forks at table and watch while she laughed and wonder what those little raisin eyes, peering out through telescopes of rattling flesh, saw that was so funny.

I never knew what poor pa was called. Never even wondered what people in the 'outside world' where he sold imported glass might call him. Perhaps they, too, called him 'poor pa' – or would they ever have believed that he might have invaded all that fat, tenderly beaten a seed bed for me to be born?

I stared at myself in a rustic mirror after my lover had gone; a big girl with a lot of yellow hair and skin and features that could only be described as excessive. Only my eyes didn't balance. I had my mother's raisin eyes.

The rotten little eyes winked at me. They were laughing, taking flight, filled with secrets. They were sexy provocative eyes that lured my mouth upward into a smile – a laugh, almost. So this is what it was like.

I left the marvellous looking-glass – more for later – and went to rummage in my suitcase, still mostly unpacked. There was a very peculiar-looking white thing, all string and lace bits, that I bought cheaply in an Indian shop, never meaning to do more than pack and unpack it. I put it on, then rope sandals, pink pearly stuff on my cheeks and ran back to the mirror to see.

Oh, I looked like a Danish pastry – golden syrup and dripping icing and impudent little raisin eyes. If poor pa could see me now. If my lover could see me now. I adjusted some strings on the dress and my breasts seemed to lunge forward, heavy with sex. I pushed them about critically as my mother would have done with a vase of gladioli. In the end I left them. They were an embarrassment, so blatant and disarrayed, but there was no going back now so I thought about the night when my laughing lover would come back and chase the darkness away with words like 'forever'.

It only seemed like forever. The night brought nothing but the dark. By ten o'clock grief had been devoured by greed. I went out in my white dress to a restaurant and chewed my way through a helplessly bleeding piece of horsemeat.

Later, when I was transfixed by a small rectangular slab of something called quince jelly, in a surgical shade of brown, he walked in. He was with a woman. His hand was laced into her meaty, sun-crisp fingers and now and again his hair touched the parched landscape of her perm. Other than that there wasn't a thing to associate them. She was old – oh, forty – and under the blue Crimplene it was all tired, spread flesh. I longed for a paperback, a postcard, a pudding of parts – God knows, even a girlfriend – to keep my eyes off them. I gazed at the seaweed on my plate seeking some depths, found none, and looked up again at the precise moment when he did.

He gave me a steady gaze – no embarrassment at all – and after quite a length turned to his fat-arse companion and whispered something. Then he stood up and came towards me, arms aloft.

'Darling, what a truly wonderful surprise,' he said. He sat himself down, kissed my hand and fondled it while grinning at me, grinning, grinning.

I held my feelings inside me in a corset of pride. 'I waited in for you tonight,' I said. 'You said you would come back.'

'Oh!' He was all serious concern. 'That's too bad, really too bad. I am so careless. I thought I had made it clear that there were things I had to do before I could attend to you.'

He ordered a bottle of pink wine, all for me, and paid for it there and then. He kissed my cheek and gave me a genuine burning stare. He said just one word. 'Soon.'

It wasn't that I minded waiting, really. I had waited so

long already. What was six, seven, eight days, except the rest of my holiday? But sitting out all alone, day after day, in the hot, fly-ridden sun, I went bad.

I was slicing tomatoes for a soup when he walked in. His grin hung over my darkness like a new moon.

'First you will feed me and then we will make love,' he said. The knife went on, biting tomato flesh, making it bleed, severing slices – a growing mound of little red grins – getting better at it all the time.

'I'm going home tomorrow,' I said. 'Too bad,' he said. His smile expanded, fit to burst. 'But tonight we will have a celebration. We will make it a night to remember.'

The knife kept my hand steady. It was entirely on my side. 'I gave you the only thing I had to offer. You took it and now it's gone,' I said.

He jabbed a finger at me. 'No baby, I gave you,' he said. His fingers dipped into the tomato slices and brought one to his mouth. 'And now I will give you something else. I will give you the truth.'

I cringed. There are things that are less than polite.

'Most of them pay for it,' he said, his grin falling off into a smirk. 'I pick out plain women and I wince when I peel off their nylon clothes and they don't wince at all when they peel off pound notes and pesetas. When I found you, you looked just drunk and desperate enough for a big bill. But I liked you. I gave it to you free. You will have golden fantasies, souvenirs, baby, that the customs men will not find when they rummage through your underthings.'

'I could kill you,' I said.

He laughed, not scared at all. 'What a savage! Cook me some food.'

The knife was my friend. It flew in the dusk like a silver bird. It was all grace. My lumpish arms, holding on, followed its flight. It knew where home was. I watched in thrilled delight as it settled like a gull in the cleft of a ravine. It held firm against the force of that scarlet waterfall; the stream of red like a human scream. My lover's face was all amazement. To have seen such sights, it seemed to say, is to have lived.

'Tell us about it.' A small claw tweaked at my cardigan. Dora had not gone away. 'Tell us about it and I'll show you what's in my box.'

In one unstoppable moment the lid was off and in another, equally as awful, my eyes had plummeted down and were scavenging the contents.

Dora's box held just one treasure. It was a finger, quite neatly severed.

Mama

William was in the garden looking at the house, which was square and yellow. Behind it and around, there was scenery; patchwork fields, cosily bumpy like an eiderdown, little hunchback shrubs, cowering in the hollows, a horizon with a tooth-edge of firs. A green vegetable, immense, William thought. He shivered in the watery warmth, feeling guilty. 'I don't think we ought to go in. The house belongs to someone,' he said.

He liked his city flat with its neat pretence of a garden where short-haired city toms stalked between the polluted flowers and a solitary bird (hired by the Tenants' Association, he said: that was his joke) gave a terse recital at eight a.m. He wrote his successful novel there and it had insulated him with the sort of superficial social life that suited him perfectly. There were parties where he could entertain people by saying nothing at all. Good-natured girls admired his writing and his grey eyes, clasped him to their marvellously assorted bodies and disappeared into cigarette smoke. Except Joanne; she married him.

She went up the three granite steps that led to the door and swept back a mass of cobwebs and thorny growths with her hands. It was a wooden door, unpainted, with a good steel knocker and two panels of glass set into the upper half. At first it appeared to be a pattern of flowers but when his eye traced the pools of plum and olive and amber, William found he was looking at a montage of faces. Joanne's fingers went out to the glass. As they did, ugly pink ridges, seeping pinpoints of blood, leaped up on her hands and wrists. 'I've never seen anything like it. It's the most beautiful house,' she said.

'Your hands . . .' William said.

She splayed her long fingers to admire them. She noticed the weals and made a noise of irritation. 'Damn brambles,' she said. William was looking absent-minded. It was a look that meant doubt. Someone seemed to borrow his bones now and then, leaving a tall pile of pale flesh to try and stand up by itself. It was a thing that had to be coped with. She arced a polished arm to hold back the brambles for him and their dappled shadow gave her a fringe.

'What am I and where am I?' she said, her face radiant with schemes. 'I don't know,' William said, which was the truth. 'Do you give up?' she said. 'No!' He bounded up the steps, ducking under rusty coils of thorn to be near her. She put her arms around his neck. 'I'm the wife of a famous writer,' she coaxed. 'I'm in *Vogue* in glorious colour in their "Writers at Home" series.'

It was Joanne who had decided that they ought to live in the country. She said he needed peace and quiet to get through his next book. There was nothing to do but agree, although a part of him niggled that the upheaval of moving house wasn't going to help him meet publishers' deadlines. It was Joanne who had spotted the house, an architectural castaway, as they drove through remote countryside in the rain, looking for tea on the way back from a weekend with friends.

'Try the door,' she said. It was meant as a dare but it sounded to William as if he had forgotten his manners. He hurled his hands at the wood. The door yielded, squealing at the assault. It carried him into the hall. She pursued him through the shadows, closing the door behind her. William wouldn't have done that.

He watched as the placid landscape diminished in the gap of the door and went black. He stood with his eyes closed, still feeling a purple sheen of sun under his eyelids, listening to Joanne's heels tapping the bare wood floor behind him in an uneven rhythm. 'This house,' she said. 'It's a dream.' She began to twirl, her heels making the sound of somebody running around a diminishing circle. 'Shh,' William said. 'Kip, kip?' her heels queried softly. Seconds dropped off into the dust. William became alarmed in case she was in a sulk. He turned abruptly.

She stood like a child, contained in a frugal stalk of sun that got in through a broken skylight. She was holding in each hand the parts of a dismembered toy. 'A doll,' she whispered. 'It's broken,' William said. Her face was a clownish mask of puzzlement! 'It's been pulled apart.' 'We'd better go,' he said. 'Wait! There's a room in there that's full of toys.' She sounded as if she was blaming him. He trotted into the room after her, almost tripping over a roller skate. 'Shit,' he muttered, kicking it. It skittered over the boards on its wheels, thudding into the side of a giant panda which collapsed without complaint.

The room seemed to be the nursery of a spoilt child. Toy soldiers and train sets, cloth toys, a tricycle, had all been touched by dust and destruction. William explored a lump of self-pity that came up in his throat. He had never had toys. He would have cared for them. 'It looks as if the people who lived here just picked up their beds and walked,' Joanne said. 'A lot of these toys are perfectly good.' William was on his knees setting to right a rocking horse. The leather ears had been tugged so hard that they stood askew on lumps of glue. 'There's something . . .' Joanne's probing was emphasized by the rapping of her shoes as she explored. 'All the windows are barred.'

The horse had been carved from a single piece of wood. Curves as smooth as skin delighted William's fingers. The glass eyes were rounded to catch the light and it gave them a nervous life. It had a real leather saddle. When he was small his father had nailed two pieces of wood together for him like a crucifix. He held the longer piece between his legs as he hopped down the lane going 'glop-glop' with his tongue against the roof of his mouth. One day the boys came down the lane and they laughed at him. In an ecstasy of rage that exhausted his whole life's supply of anger, he had raised his horse above his head and hacked about him until they were a red blur in his tears and their blood.

'William.' Joanne's voice crumbled from her lungs like sand from a bank. He gave the horse a reassuring pat to say he would be back and went to look for his wife. She was standing in another doorway, not posed for an entrance but artlessly, feet apart like a middle-aged woman. He heard the other noise. 'Mama.' It sounded like one of those dolls with a mechanical box set into the body that emits a wail when you turn it upside down. Joanne's clenched fingers were empty. A child? William forced his feet to perform a man's heavy step, needing the reassuring sound. On the bare planks his steps sounded villainous so he tiptoed to the door trying not to be put out at the way Joanne's body jerked when the sound came again. 'Mama.'

There was a man in the room. He sat in a little pink wicker chair. He was dressed in a flannel nightshirt and looked like an invalid. His skin had a sticky texture and he was stunted in height like a midget, but fat. He billowed over the basket-work. William picked a path through a dusty jumble of toys, looking out for the doll that had given such alarm to his wife, seeing only his own shadow which seemed somehow less substantial than the other shadow that spanned the floor like the legs of a giant spider; the bars on the window. He attempted a smile. The man, watching him, seemed to expect more. His eyes were like withered figs. 'I'm sorry.' William was miserable with embarrassment. 'The front door was open. We'll go.'

Joanne, who had followed him with the teetering steps of a geisha, gave one small jerk when the door slammed. For an instant they watched it mistrustfully, then stepped forward together and exchanged a nervous smile as both their hands shot out for the knob. 'It's stuck,' William said, testing it. He worried it exploratively. He gave an energetic tug. 'Jammed.' The man was watching them with a pleased intentness. 'Warped!' William called out to him. 'Must be damp.' There was no damp in the house. He had checked on that. His hands were damp, his forehead.

He wanted to cope with the situation, to make Joanne proud of him. He stamped across the room, knowing there must be a sensible answer and dinner somewhere in a nice hotel with a fire lit. He crouched in front of the little man. 'Old doors,' he said, 'do that all the time. It takes a bit of know-how to open them.' The man's dusty eyes conceded nothing. Behind, the nagging of the brass door knob as Joanne persisted, sounded like a criticism.

The noise stopped. 'William!' The titter of Joanne's heels, her voice high with relief. 'William, it's open.' He basked as her cool fingers greeted his hand. Another hand, not cool and familiar but monstrous, flew out and severed their union. The fat man's fingers manacled Joanne's wrist. 'Mama,' he said again. He was pawing at her. 'Don't do that.' William's voice hardened hopefully. 'Mama,' the man whimpered. Joanne shuddered. His hand tightened. A bloodless band on her wrist framed his fingers. She looked to William for help. He couldn't meet her eyes. He dropped his gaze instead to the fingers locked on to her arm.

There was no escape for him. He felt that. The house was not civilized. It wanted to strip him. In the slow, sedated moments of shock the man in the chair became him, holding on to his mother's wrist, his small, tearing nails catching in the clunking chains of her bracelet. He had developed an ear for despair on the delicate chatter of the metal links. Each night when her bracelet went on, she went out. Once he had tried to stop her. 'Mama,' he had cried, catching her wrist. She had jerked away, shock and revulsion in her face – Joanne's face. 'Your mama,' Joanne said, taking a deep breath to steady her voice, 'went to the shops.' He looked up quickly but she was speaking to the man. 'She's at the door now. I'm going to let her in.' She attempted to stand. The man would not let her. 'He knows the hall door is open. I told him,' William said uselessly.

'Your mama,' Joanne said, 'went hours ago. It's beginning to get dark outside. She's walking through a forest and she's frightened. Unless we go and find her she's never coming back. You'll be all alone.'

He understood. He sighed and let go her wrist. It was a child's comprehension, understanding the moment but believing it to be eternal. Like most women, Joanne thought it was all right to do anything so long as it was for the best. For a moment she hovered, waiting for the right instinct of disciplined kindness. 'Mama!' the man cried, flinging his arms around her so that her breath came out in choking gulps. He buried his head against her breast. Over the top of his baby skull her face was almost a caricature of horror. Her hands were held outward stiffly as though in supplication, although it was really to keep some part of herself free from contact. William launched himself at the man, slapping his head, tugging on his shoulders. The man's hands went to Joanne's neck. She sobbed in fright. William clawed at the obese paws. They had turned to iron. 'Go!' Joanne whispered at him. He remained where he was, crouched and stiff with shock. 'Get someone,' she begged. He scurried to the door, almost made it. His foot was mocked by another roller skate. He tripped.

He put out a hand to save himself. The toy steered playfully into his fingers. His fist clenched around it. He leaped to his feet without a thought and charged back across the room hearing with mild surprise the noise as the metal bar and wheels struck the bald man's skull. The man rolled back in his chair. The basketwork gave an endless groan.

'You've killed him,' Joanne said. William's voice shuddered: 'Let's get out of here.' He took his wife's hand and helped her to her feet. Without looking back, they went to the door, walking to pretend it was quite normal. William opened the door. 'There,' he said. When he moved aside to allow his wife to pass, a freak draught caught at the door and swung it shut with a venomous crash. He grasped the knob. It was stuck fast. 'I ... can't ...' His voice rose on the edge of panic. He didn't like being locked in a room with a corpse. 'Let me.' Joanne pushed him aside and wrestled with the knob. For five seconds while her small body attacked the jammed door he resisted the temptation. On the sixth, he turned.

The man was grinning at the door. A trickle of blood was allowed to wander unchecked down the side of a nose like a mushroom and over his petulant little mouth. William touched his wife with stiff fingers. She glanced back irritably, then froze. 'We've lost,' she whispered. 'No, darling,' William said, horrified. 'He knows this house and its draughts. He's mocking us. There's nothing he can do to us. We'll find a way out.' He reached for her hand. She swatted it. 'Stay here,' she commanded. 'You don't understand this. You'll have to leave it to me.' Her voice had that tight edge of irritation that he dreaded. 'Oh, Jo,' he pleaded. 'I read about a case like this once,' she said. 'There was a man with one hugely developed area of his brain that gave him ... powers ... and crushed his other mental faculties.' 'Where did you read it?' 'Christ, I don't know, what does it matter? Maybe it was a film.' William sighed. 'What does it matter?' 'Don't patronize me,' Joanne said. Her voice was hard. 'If this is left to you and your logical thinking God knows what will happen. We'll be found by someone, someday, covered in dust like the toys.' The things she said frightened William. His anxieties engulfed him.

'Oh, for Christ's sake, don't look like that,' she said contemptuously. 'One ghoul's quite enough for any room.' He gripped the door knob, cool and solid. He could not feel anything except the knob and the ache in his throat. He was an amoeba suspended about the knob, a vapour. 'He probably can't actually move objects or he would certainly have put on a cabaret,' she mused energetically, 'but he can certainly direct natural elements, draughts, say. He must have incredible concentration. Our only hope is to break it. He's got to have a weakness. I'm going to try and find out what it is and hold his attention long enough for you to open the door. Whatever I do, don't move. And keep trying the door.'

He felt an unpleasant admiration for the efficient way in which she went to the little man, wiped at his bleeding face with a handkerchief and then caressed his head and the sides of his face. She was whispering in his ear. He watched her warily for a time and then put out a hand to touch her face. He smiled. His hand dropped to her body and moved over her breast. He grinned.

William commenced a desperate and monotonous dragging on the door knob. In the background he could hear Joanne's voice like a stream of honey. He tugged at the knob harder, louder, hoping to drown out her voice but the words came at him like figures in a nightmare. The clatter of the brass fitting was the sound of a spectre in chains. William no longer held any hope. He knew that this was his life and he furiously performed his function of joggling the archaic knob, not with the smallest hope of escape but to divide Joanne's attention.

The noise he made was so relentless that he was not aware of the moment when she stopped speaking. She was eyeing the man with that expression of hers, her arms folded as precisely as laundry. 'I give up,' she said quietly. In that instant it became evident that the whole house depended on her. The man scoured her face for some sign of leniency. Shadows lengthened in the room. 'I'm leaving,' she said.

The man, crafty, glued his eyes on the door. 'Don't try

159

your tricks,' she warned. She grabbed him by the shoulders and shook him like a rat. He lowered his eyes. William tried the door surreptitiously. It was stuck fast. 'I can walk out any time I want,' Joanne was saying. 'I would like you to open the door.' The man was confused. He rattled his chair. Joanne smiled and stroked his gashed head. 'There.' She bent and kissed his mouth, allowing his hands to fondle her. 'Like!' the man said. She offered him a coy look of reproach and glanced at the door. The man's face crumpled in angry disappointment. 'Open the door,' Joanne commanded. He glared at her. His jaws trembled with rage. 'Open it?' she said in a voice that played like water on stone. She came and sat on his knee, placed his hands on her breasts. She began to undo the buttons of her blouse.

William, punishing the door in his agitation, found that it was open. He blinked at the dusky hall through his tears, surprised at its provincial ordinariness. Through the glass panels in the hall door he could make out the hump of his own car.

He could leave now – alone – drive until he came to a hotel and have hot whisky sent to his room. A deep bed, feathering him with oblivion; morning heralded by discreet knuckles on the door and a girl with fat legs bringing the comfortable smells of toast and coffee and her own sweat. He reeled at the homeliness of the fantasy.

'Aah,' said the man. William whirled. He spun the door so that it hopped into its lock. 'Nooo!' he howled.

Joanne and the man, piled up on the wicker seat like children in an absurd nursery game, turned faces surprised and guilty. Irritation quickly claimed his wife's features. 'I thought I told you not to move,' she said. 'Get back to the door.' Her eyes, darting, groped about for some memory hastily flung in her brain. 'The door!' she exclaimed. 'I heard it slam.' Her eyes burned with accusation. 'It was open. You slammed the door.'

'I had to stop you,' his voice gurgled with tears. 'He's a man. You can't do that.'

Joanne slid from her perch, managing not to look foolish. 'So he's a man,' she sneered. 'Mr Universe.' The man looked uneasy. He split his face into a boy's smile of ingratiation. Joanne wheeled on William. 'What would you know about it?' He backed away. She pursued him. 'You don't look much of a man to me – more like a grubby child. If I leaned on you, I'd squash you like an insect. As a man you only exist on the page. You're the real monster. A paper monster! How white you are!'

William concentrated on trying to stop the tears. 'You're disgusting,' Joanne said. 'Wipe your dirty nose.'

He had to stop crying. She was terribly cross. He caught his cuff in his fingers and slid his sleeve under his nose, searching in his mind for happy things to dam this abysmal waterfall.

The things he found in there were terrible; school reports, forgotten birthdays, murderous boys. He was tired. It was wrong to be on one's feet in the dark, people's faces eaten away by shadows, distorting without warning into nightmare shapes. He didn't like the dark. A bolt of blue steel attacked the shadows, brave and good like King Arthur's sword. He fixed his eyes on the glittering shaft. A crossbar! Crikey! It was a bicycle. Why hadn't he noticed it before? It was a beaut.

He revoked his tears with a snort and scrubbed his face with the back of his hand. He swam in the shadows, his eyes seeing everything, holding back the night. At his age they should. He gripped the cycle in his hands. Wow! Five gears and a Duraluminum frame. He swung a leg over the crossbar and eased his buttocks on to the saddle. Worship filled his lungs. His toes bit at the pedals, enjoying their friskiness. 'Giddyup!' He set them orbiting like chairoplanes.

His suspended foot captured one flying pedal and drove it earthward, his other foot tackling its ascending twin with ease. The wheels surged. Around, around, around he flew, wobbling just a bit as the bike negotiated strewn objects, sometimes not bothering to steer but enjoying the sensation as he squashed some silly toy. The wheels, squeaking from lack of oil, cried 'whee!'

'Stop it!' Joanne's voice grazed like gunshot. He slowed down, pleased with the new sound the wheels made, like grating laughter. Her voice ranted over his lovely noise: 'This is too much. I'm finished with you. If we get out of here alive, I'm leaving you. Are you listening?' He was not listening. He would not. He cycled faster. Her voice was on a pitch with the hyena shrieks of his wheels. 'As for you –' she rounded on the man who sat quite still in the chair, boneless hands enveloping the wicker arms like pastry – 'no wonder no one likes you. No wonder you're all alone. Dirty, disgusting, untidy . . .'

'Not,' said the man with small defiance. She stormed over and slapped his wrist. He began to snivel. 'I know how to deal with you,' she said. 'I'll make you sorry for your tricks. Stupid boy!' She began picking up the toys with frenzied efficiency, deftly avoiding the bicycle wheels, stacking the toys in a neat heap in the corner, out of harm's way. As she crouched by the door, scooping up pieces of Meccano, she found she was able to identify the colours of the parts; green, yellow, blue. She watched, mesmerized, as it advanced towards her, spilling over her hands, her toes – a pool of light. She looked up. The door was opening. A shaft of moonlight climbed in from the skylight in the hall. The door opened quite wide. She looked back with a start. The man was watching the door, urging it open, wider, wider.

'William!' An excited shout. 'We're free. Oh, honey, I did it. Let's go!' She smiled as the gleaming metal came towards her; with surprise as the machine began to circle around her, closing in, round and round and round.

'Oh, William,' she said gently. 'Don't be silly. Come on.'

Round and round, faster, faster, making her skip a bit to

avoid injury. 'William,' she said angrily. In the moonlight his face was terribly intense. His grey eyes stared at the door. 'Wheee!' went the wheels. 'William!' Joanne screamed. Crash! went the door.

He pedalled slowly from her. She ran to the door. She knew, she knew but she tried anyway. She crept into a corner and huddled there.

'Mama.' It sounded quite far away, quite faint. She covered her ears with her hands. 'Ma-ma.' Closer. She could hear the clumsy shuffle across the floor. She tried to back away, pressing into the wall. In the dark he might not find her. A sound of fright tore loose from her throat. Something touched her. 'William!' she screamed.

He felt proud to be there when she needed him. They needed each other. Now she would never go away. Joanne's heart began to pound at the same time as her body started to respond to the familiarity of the hand reaching for her in the dark. 'Mama,' William smiled.

The Complete Angler

'I grew up in the city,' Ormond said. 'Everything around me was dirty and dry. I began to dream about water.'

It wasn't as if he lived in the desert. There was rain and second-hand bath-water; taupe dishwater creeping with fried leftovers and puddles emulsified with mud and suspicious objects. He dreamed about oceans and rivers, vast, clean expanses of blue where he would bathe or float. He never knew what it was like to drift and dive, warm and weightless, until . . .

'Didn't you have any hobbies?' Bernadette said.

With his eyes closed he couldn't imagine what she was thinking so he forced himself to look at her and was shocked by the shape of her face, lapsed on the pillow. 'I collected stamps.'

'Stamp collecting, you poor little prick,' she yelped.

He told her all about himself, surprised at the eagerness with which he stripped to the bone, flesh and fantasy, for her inspection.

He didn't think she was listening because after a time she turned to him and asked him if he had ever thought about fishing.

Ormond Sedge was dreadful in bed. He knew he was dreadful because Chrissie had told him: and Chrissie was his wife. Six months after they were married she had begun to tell their friends. She called him 'poor Ormond' because it gave the telling a sympathetic ring; but 'poor' in her own mind because he had failed to endow her with libidinous riches. Their friends minded being told that poor Ormond had reached a new low, as if he was the pound. It divided their loyalties, both between Chrissie and Ormond and with their own partners. If a woman sided with Chrissie it was saying she understood, which came out as a criticism of whatever man bore responsibility for her orgasms. The man who offered Ormond a reassuring wink across the room was seen to be beaconing signals of sexual distress.

The one who minded least was Ormond. He sat in a corner, smiling, and basked in the glow of pink her raspberry-coloured satin shirt threw on her pale skin, making her seem luscious with frustration. When her arms rose in irritation he admired the effect of perfect, ornamental breasts pressed against the thin fabric of her clothes and counted the hours until he could be in bed with her again.

Chrissie lay absolutely flat in the bed, defensively dead like a cat that is being patted by children. 'You'll have to hurry up,' she said crossly. 'I've got to work in the morning.'

'Coming,' he called out with gay insincerity. He knew he had stayed too long. He would come out in a minute. He would come out as soon as the pleasure diminished. He was floating. Tropical waters lapped his mouth. A Pacific whirl-pool sucked at his groin. By moving very gently he could make tiny waves but he had to avoid sudden movements or there would be an end. If the end was death he might take a chance. It was a small injury, nothing to speak of. It left one disarmed, diminished, excluded.

Once, when he was very small, he had been taken to the sea and the ocean was all gone. 'Silly boy, the tide has gone out,' people said when he summoned witnesses to the catas-trophe. He put on his bathing knickers and squatted like a frog on the coils of parched purple weed, spiked with shells and skeletons, that set apart the portions of the earth where creatures swam or walked. Hours he sat there, clawed by wet winds and terrified by sudden small eruptions in the sand until, like a frog, he went green. The water came back but it was not enough to know that these things happen every day.

'Ormond,' said an oracle. He opened his eyes just wide enough to look at Chrissie's lips. It was lovely to be called Ormond by a woman who had a mouth like a plum. He took a small dive from sheer elation. A little breeze sighed and whispered, stronger than he'd expected because it pushed a shudder right through his body. He took a deep breath and held himself very still. Everything went dead calm. He grinned in relief.

When she saw him smiling she pulled her plummy lips down into a droop and jerked away from him. 'You'll have to get yourself a mistress,' she said.

It was hardly any trouble finding a mistress. The bars were full of single women who paid for some of their drinks and sat with legs shaped for cello practice. The difficulty, Ormond discovered, lay in persuading a girl that she ought not merely to be a mistress in general but a mistress in particular. To a person. To him actually.

He spent a week tapping girls on the shoulder, hoping their faces wouldn't horrify when they swished their shiny hair to get a look at him. He spent a lot of money on Pimms and Martinis. He was getting nowhere.

'I want to ask your advice,' he said to a girl called Virgin, who had fascinating white eyelashes and small breasts that pointed through her chiffon tabard like ballet slippers. 'Gin and lime,' she advised, handing him her glass.

'If you were a man how would you set about getting a mistress?' Ormond signalled the barman for a fresh glass of fluorescent. 'You're looking for someone to screw,' the girl said helpfully. 'No, not exactly. I'm married,' Ormond boasted. 'It's my wife who wants the mistress. In fact she insists on it.'

'Your wife wants a mistress?' Virgin said. 'Gosh.'

In the end he had to settle for Bernadette, whose make-up

had a look of boiled butterscotch sauce; whose figure was warm yeast rising under skimpy damp satin; who was a lot older than anybody. If she wasn't exactly what he had in mind, she allowed him no time for consideration. Shortly after he had introduced himself he found that he was standing naked in her bedroom, marooned on an island on his own clothing which her deft, typist's fingers had unleashed to his feet as raddled anchors. She twiddled his genitals as if they were a squeaky toy to make him chuckle and bundled him into bed, tucking herself around him like a duvet.

'How was it?' he asked. With his eyes closed he liked Bernadette. She had an affectionate scent and a magnificent foreign tidal swell. It was like going on holidays. 'How was it?' he whispered in her ear. She felt quite limp in his arms and when he touched her face her mouth was open. His heart began to thud in case she was ill or dead but she groaned and turned over and said 'Christ' and he laughed at his foolishness. She had only been asleep. 'My wife thinks I lack technique,' he told her when she was properly awake, and she laughed like a dolphin.

He told her about growing up in the city, his visit to the seaside. Then one day in a stranger's house in a dark room at a party, he had found himself entering a woman. His whole body seemed engulfed in warm, fluid depths and he could smell the salt. With his eyes closed he could make a picture, a child's painting of a seaside scene. Salt and searing blues met on a scalloped horizon where a grapefruit sun bounced. Three linear gulls were piped on to the sky. On the ocean, quite close to land, a boy floated, as light and as nice and as brown as a biscuit. Ormond knew there was something called a climax. He had no wish in his life for climaxes – only an absence of irritation; but the girl beneath him joggled so fiercely that he had to concentrate just to keep his balance. She vacuumed him relentlessly while he sobbed that he loved her. Just as he was burrowing into sleep she snapped on the light. He had to look at her blotched face and tell her she was lovely. 'Thank you,' he had said. For teaching him a lesson.

It was then that Bernadette asked him about fishing. She lit a cigarette and propped up her breasts in a nest of sheets, considerate of their age. 'I was thinking,' she said. 'Lakes and rivers can be just as pretty as the seaside. Fishermen spend a lot of time in the water.'

He couldn't seem to grasp what she was talking about. He tried to focus on her but her whole appearance seemed to have slid sideways. She clucked her fuzzy mouth in a gesture of impatience and heaved herself out on to the floor, her big, naked backside looking oddly innocent as she ploughed across the carpet, full of purpose. It was most confusing. She was rummaging in a bureau. She turned to him, smiling with success. She had got herself a book. 'If you're bored I'll go,' he said, but she paid no attention, merely crashed back into bed again and began leafing through the pages as if it was a dictionary and she was seeking a phrase in a foreign language. After a time the pages stopped whirling and she began to read. 'For Christ's sake,' she said several times with interest, as her garbled features settled into intelligent repose.

'... *And for that I shall tell you, that in ancient times a debate hath risen, and it remains yet unresolved, whether the happiness of man in this world doth consist more in contemplation or action?*' came the words of Izaak Walton through the bruised lips of Bernadette. '*Concerning which, some have endeavoured to maintain their opinion of the first; by saying, that the nearer we mortals come to God by way of imitation, the more happy we are.*

'*And they say, that God enjoys himself only, by a contemplation of his own infiniteness, eternity, power, and goodness, and the like.*

'*And on the contrary, there want not men of equal authority and credit, that prefer action to be the more excellent; as namely, experiments in physick, and the application of it, both for the ease and prolongation of man's life; by which each man is enabled to act and to do good to others, either to serve his country or to do good to particular persons.*

'*Concerning which two opinions I shall forbear to add a third, by declaring my own; and rest contented in telling you, my very worthy friend, that both these meet together, and do most properly belong to the most honest, ingenuous, quiet and harmless art of angling.*'

In the days that followed Ormond contemplated. He contemplated art and virtue and the maintenance of human society. He contemplated doing good to particular persons for the ease and prolongation of life. When the time came, he contemplated his grease-painted mistress, sitting up in bed with no clothes on, reading her book. Her big, aquatic eyes bulged at him affectionately and a tranquil stream of sweat meandered through her breasts. 'Hi there, Pisceator,' she said. When he moved to the bed to kiss her she disappeared beneath the sheets. He dived in after her and rolled on top of her musky bulk. She squirmed away with strength and determination. 'I'm a fish,' she gurgled. 'You've frightened me.'

She taught him how fishes had to be surprised, tricked, teased, baited. '*First let your bait be as big a red worm as you can find,*' she read out, diligent as Mr Chips, '*without a knot.*'

She planted the book on his chest and slid down on him to prepare the bait. It was an action that caused Ormond to re-think his entire philosophy. He wondered if there was something he ought to be doing but he didn't like to interrupt her, so he began to read. '*Note also,*' he read, '*that when the worm is well baited, it will crawl up and down as far as the lead will give, with much enticeth the fish to bite without suspicion.*' His exhilaration was more scientific than sexual when her teeth explored flesh and nipped him daintily. He continued on, finding his own instruction. '*Having thus* prepared your baits, and fitted your tackling, repair to the river . . .'

'And you must fish for him with a strong line and not a little hook,' Bernadette instructed, reading on over his livid left ear.

'And let him have time to gorge your hook.' Her voice began to go funny. 'Then when you have a bite, you shall perceive the top of your float to sink suddenly into the water . . . then strike gently and hold your rod at a bent a little while; but if you both pull together you are sure to lose your game.' He wasn't going to lose his game. He was winning. Twice she had lost her place in the book, and when she found it her recital came out with sounds like a church organ being tuned. '. . . then mark where he plays most and stays longest,' she continued valiantly. '. . . and there, or thereabouts, at a clear bottom and a convenient landing-place, take one of your angles ready fitted as aforesaid, and sound the bottom which should,' she finished with a tremendous amount of noise, 'be eight or ten feet deep.'

Bernadette was a big fish. Landing her left him drenched and exhausted. Weariness pinned him to his pillow. It dragged his hair down and numbed his toes but before the first snores chugged laboriously up his lungs, he was an amazed witness to the spectacle of his spirit dancing like a two-year-old with a fisherman's thrill for the one that didn't get away.

In the weeks that followed Ormond began modestly to believe that he was acquiring some skill as an angler. It was easy to strike with a singing heart in such a yielding stream. Once, for practice, he pretended he was with Chrissie. His mind sketched her deceptively languid face and round pouting mouth. Her eyes flew open, gentian blue, brimming with spite. 'You call that bait?' she hissed. 'I call it bird food.' He clung to his mistress and babbled his apprehension. Bernadette ruffled his hair and looked for her book. She read him some lines of a poem.

> '*The jealous trout, that low did lie,*
> *Rose at a well-dissembled flie.*
> *There stood my Friend, with patient skill,*
> *Attending of his trembling quill.*'

'Sir Henry Wotton wrote that,' she said, adding as a reprimand: 'He was over seventy.'

There were days when Bernadette's whole body looked tousled as she groped in the bed for her handbook. '*Observe, lastly,*' she read in a cracked whisper following a spectacular siege that neglected several suns and moons, '*that after three or four days' fishing together, your game will be very shy and wary, and you shall hardly get above a bite or two at a baiting; then your only way is to desist from your sport, about two or three days.*'

'Couldn't you just say no?' he teased.

'I couldn't say no,' she told him. 'I love you too much.'

She looked at him guiltily, her eyes already receding behind a screen of water; his big, sad, scaly catch. His catch. What did one do with a catch? It had not cropped up anywhere in his tuition. It was a problem, especially as he felt he was near to graduation. Lately he had found himself eyeing Chrissie's hard little hostile bottom and longing to sound it. He would simply explain to Bernadette. She was not after all, a child; nor even a fish.

He told her it was time for him to go back to his wife. The words seemed to make no sense to her. That was the arrangement, he reminded her gently. It had been understood from the beginning. She shook her head until it threatened to disconnect. He couldn't remember, actually, if he had explained to Bernadette or merely told all the other mistresses. He felt there ought to be a way to finish things nicely. It occurred to him that he lacked technique.

'If there's something I've done wrong ...' The plea leaped from her and bounced around the walls in ramshackle desperation. When he could no longer stand the raw look of her he dropped his gaze. His eye connected with an open page of the book, thrust into his hands earlier for the initiation of their sport; and there it was. '... *which I tell you, that you may the better believe that I am certain, if I catch a Trout in one meadow, he shall be white and faint, and very like to be lousy:*' he recited with feeling. '*And, as certainly, if I catch a Trout in the next meadow, he shall be strong, and red, and lusty, and much better meat.*' His voice rose with emotion, with gratitude, with overwhelming lust for his wife. '*Trust me, scholar, I have caught many a Trout in one particular meadow, that the very shape and enamelled colour of him hath been such as hath joyed me to look on him: and I have then, with much pleasure, concluded with Solomon, "Everything is beautiful in his season."*'

For some reason Bernadette seemed to be coming to pieces. It must have been to do with her age. The tears appeared to be melting her face. He was eager to be on his way and forget her. 'I'll never forget you,' he told a palette of running colours. 'You led me through troubled waters, like Moses.'

'Sure,' she sniffed. 'Grandma Moses.' He left her then, rolled up in her ivory satin sheets like Neapolitan ice-cream dripping down a cornet.

It was a week before he was ready. There were library books to be read. They didn't tell you everything. He had to ring Bernadette to clear up one point. She was surprisingly good about it. Chrissie could sense a change. 'Have you got yourself a mistress? Have you?' she demanded repeatedly as he was poised at the washbowl with his toothbrush or standing with one leg in his pyjamas or collapsing over the edge of a dream.

'Yes,' he answered, grinning to himself under the blankets on the seventh day. She was silent while she delicately packaged herself in the bed beside him. 'What's she like?' she asked. Ormond began to laugh. 'She's fat and ugly,' he chortled. 'She's the ugliest woman I've ever seen.'

Chrissie beat him savagely. 'You liar,' she shouted, showering him with knuckles. He faced her, risking blows on the nose. She looked so beautiful. 'Do you love her?' she asked, leaning over him with raised fists. 'I'm ... grateful to her,' he said. She made a dreary noise, a snort. Her arms fell to her sides and she dropped down in the bed like a stone. He wanted to take her in his arms but he had been too well tutored. 'Surprise, trick, tease, bait,' his mind recited obediently while he waited for his wife to go off her guard. She snorted again. 'Poor little lamb,' he thought full of compassion until an explosion of sound broke loose from her lungs; not sobs but unkind laughter. 'You nearly had me there, toad-face,' she spluttered. 'You really made me jealous. So help me, I married a deceitful weevil. Did you think I'd believe you got yourself a mistress? Virgin brides are ten a penny but with a mistress you've got an entrance examination to pass.'

For an answer, he sat up and started to sing in a solemn, dusty voice.

'And when the timorous Trout I wait
To take, and he devours my bait,
How poor a thing, sometimes I find,
Will captivate a greedy mind.'

Chrissie had not shared bed and book with Bernadette. Nor was she much given to the classics. It was understandable that she had never heard of 'The Angler's Song.' She did what anyone would have done in her position, lay there gaping with her mouth open, exactly like a fish. Ormond seized his moment. He swooped and kissed her open mouth, not hungrily but merrily, dartingly, like a fly over the surface of a lake on a summer evening. His lips lighted on her breast, her knee, the sole of her foot, with the idle delight and presumption of a Mayfly who has just a day to live.

His tongue was the feather of a partridge, the feather of a black drake. He lapped her with the harle of a peacock's tail; teased her with the wings of a buzzard and the small feathers of speckled fowl. When all the scorn had fallen from her body and she lay trembling like a leaf waiting to be taken by the wind, he heard the sly voice of Izaak Walton in his ear: *'Thus have a jury of flies, likely to betray and condemn all the Trouts in the river.'*

Having thus prepared his baits, and fitted his tackling, he repaired to the river. *'First let your rod be light, and very gentle,'* he remembered, but later, *'you must fish with a strong line.'* He knew how to tease a fish. He had developed an old fisherman's instinct and understood the exact moment for sounding the bottom. He had a bite! Her breath came in faltering sighs, quite separate from the violence of her body. 'I love you,' she sang. 'Oh, I love you.' It was a violin solo borne up to heaven on the impossible notes of an orgasm, accompanied by orchestral movements from her body. 'My darling,' Ormond said with triumph and, just before he picked her up by the amazed hair and smashed her head very hard against the brass bedpost, 'My catch!'

She was dead. He never meant to hurt her, he explained to her surprised body, telling her he loved her, trying to make her understand. It was simply the thing that one did with a catch when it had been landed and was floundering and gasping, out of its element; a part of the angler's code. Bernadette had told him.

The Cage

She had developed a hawk eye for young girls in love. She became a collector of their smiles; the gift of beauty that broke out on the plainest face. They never even knew. She had not known. Only afterwards, when she was grey and drained of spirit as a rat, had she seen that smile on another woman's face and recognized it and fury built up inside her like bricks as if the woman had stolen it from her and wore it in the street and didn't care who knew.

Even now she found herself from habit, spying on a girl who was impelled by love, bright with vision. Men followed you when you wore that smile. She turned her head to watch the transmuted woman's progress in the street and from the rear she presented only a behind of clay in jeans and espadrilles with flailing soles. She sat back in the taxi and caught a detail of her own face in the driver's mirror; a grown-up face, well-kept and cleverly groomed; a face hollowed out and filled with light as a Hallowe'en pumpkin, and fleeting across it – a smile.

When the letter came in the morning she had spread it out beside her breakfast and looked at it for a long time. She did not have to read the words. She had written them at the back of her head a long time ago. She tried to picture him writing them and then for the first time she realized that she no longer had to draw fantasy for company; she had something to do. She got up and dressed herself and methodically set about phone calls and letters to put her life in order.

They did not fall in love, she thought, like other people. They met and recognized each other and were relieved. On the day they met they had talked together for a while and then the unlikely thought struck her: 'What a pity he's not more handsome. I could live with this man.' A few minutes later she said something that made him laugh and she thought how much she liked his face and that above anything else she could not bear to live without that face.

Sometimes, after she had lost him, his face came into her mind and pain swept over her like a plague. She tried to be sensible. She fenced the pain, telling herself he was not the man she knew; he was older, less fanciful, with bits of other people's lives stuck all over him. She knew hardly anything about him now. She no longer knew if she loved him. The pain was still there but she could not tell if it was love or the loss of love or just the knowledge that nothing would ever be like it again.

After their affair he kept in touch. She was grateful to him for leaving her his hand to hold for she was in the dark and she was terrified. Sometimes she felt guilty for the demands she made on him and worried that she might damage his life with her claim. Then she told herself that it was he who had lost his way and needed her hand to guide him. She could not believe that he no longer loved her. She thought he did not know how to proceed with love and was compelled, again and again, to return to its starting point.

If she kept faith, if he kept touch, they would still be on the same paths when he found the skill or altered his view of life. He telephoned her once a week and she poured out for him the insipid distillation of her days. After a year or so her life ran out. 'You need a change,' he said kindly. She took it as an order and went to live abroad.

When she first arrived in Paris she was a cupboard creature, timid and scuttling, crumpling the diplomas which declared her a designer in a manner that doomed her to dressmaker. Paris is full of such women. It likes them. Their work is excellent and they pursue it twelve hours a day. They do not challenge the style of clients nor tempt their husbands. After a few years the diligence of her work made her successful and this in turn gave her confidence. She established her own small salon. She became attractive in the Parisian manner. She was chic. Some people thought her hard.

Occasionally she took a lover. She did not do this from passion or frivolity but in the way a sensible woman goes to her doctor for a check-up. She wanted to make sure that all the bits were in proper order and capable of the right responses. She was completely unaware of feelings in these men. She could look quite coldly on the lamenting eyes and piteous mouths that complained 'je t'aime'. Love was what she felt for him, what he had once felt for her. It was unconnected to any other man.

In any case her mind was too full to accommodate the intrusion of the strangers who visited her bed. He still kept in touch with her. He came to Paris to see her, not often, but three or four times a year. He said he came because of business. There was always a section of his visit x'd off to prove it. 'Now I'm yours,' he would say when that was disposed of. 'Tell me about you.'

She saved up all the stories of her life to make it sound amusing or absurd. The events of her life only came to life in the telling for him. It was worth it. It made him smile. She was happy then. She could not see him smiling and not be happy.

She always hoped he would say something before he went away again. Not just anything; she was demanding. 'I miss you.' 'I love you.' 'Come home.' Instead he said, in rationed tones, after kissing her forehead: 'Take care. I'll see you soon.'

When he was gone she felt the pieces of herself drifting away in great gouts of loneliness, leaving her raw, half-eaten, helpless. She was a planet out of orbit tearing around in black outer space, spinning, unravelling, leaving a trail of herself burning and dying; nothing dramatic, just a flickering dot on the great isolation of the firmament. But she was not alone. Soon after he left her, they came, leaping up around her like the flames of candles, the people of his life.

Once he told her how he had given a woman a book she was looking for, had come up behind her while she was cooking and surprised her with it. She became devoted to this small sequence, playing it over and over in her mind; the kind of woman who would want that book, the meal she was cooking for him, the serving of intellectual and physical interests which pointed to a wider range of pleasures shared and gratified. She had to acquaint herself with the woman, ally herself to her, or the pain would kill her. She thought that nothing would ever hurt as much as that.

She did not always use her imagination to keep up with his life. Sometimes she became a detective, telephoning people who knew him and cunningly introducing his name. 'Guess who he's going out with now?' she would say playfully. Five times out of six the person at the other end obliged with a woman's name and once, horrifyingly, the woman to whom she was speaking said: 'Don't, Anna, don't tease. I love him.' All in all she had a quite full life.

There was an occasion when he came to see her and whisked her off to a hotel in the country. In the car he looked ahead but he kept taking his hand off the wheel to touch her. After several hundred kilometres she leaned back and sighed deeply and dismissed all the pain because she knew that he was going to stay with her. But in the hotel, which was a manor in a forest, he put her away from him in a room along miles of corridor and when they ate or drank did not sit next to her but studied her under various angles of candle and lamp light. One morning when she was in bed, drinking coffee, he came in and dived upon her and kissed her passionately and then he went and looked at himself in a mirror and seemed quite satisfied. 'I'm getting married,' he told her.

The relief she felt was enormous.

'I didn't want to tell you on the phone,' he said.

'You should get married,' she said. 'It will be good for you.'

She learned to live with her injuries and was cheerful as a cripple. She got herself a little dog which she did not like but might learn to love. The mists of girlhood blew away from her and she emerged a woman, quite clear sighted. As an alternative to the ornate images that had filled her head she spun around herself an environment of great fancy. Her bedroom was full of little pictures and lace and a great white bed which no one was permitted to mess up except the dog. She still occasionally saw men but she no longer engaged in the routine of passion. She was surprised, in a passionless way, to note that one of the men who had been a lover now remained as her friend. She observed also that the other man, the only man, was no longer at the centre of her life. She still felt an ache when he visited her mind, but it was, with the rest of her, diluted. She could even smile sometimes to think that he was now, at last, a married man.

But he was not. He wrote to her six months later. He was still, he joked, a hopeless bachelor. He was coming to Paris. He would like to see her.

'Yes,' she wrote back and was instantly unhinged. Feeling flooded back into her in such measure that it made her dizzy. With the selfishness of lovers she was compelled to talk about him. She called up the man who had become her friend and told him to come over. She gave him dinner and he was forced to eat it against a cruel narrative which excluded him.

'I thought I had lost him,' she said at last, 'but he is coming to see me.'

'You cannot lose him,' her friend reassured her. She smiled at him in gratitude but then she saw from the directness of his look that he was going to punish her. He was playing with matchsticks, making them into a shape on the table. 'You are in a cage. You live your life through the bars of a cage.

it. Sometimes he will come and look at you and sometimes he will not bother. On good days he will throw you crumbs and on bad days he might forget. He may even take you out on his hand but you will not fly away.' He tried to put his arms around her when he saw tears on her face but she was angry and she beat him off. He touched her hair. His compassion was maddening. 'You have forgotten how to fly,' he judged, 'and you are sad as all caged birds are.'

'I am not sad,' she cried. 'I am so happy. Why do you spoil my happiness?' After she had got rid of him she sat down on her bed and tugged impatiently at the ear of her little dog, and waited.

He came with a book for her, of Victorian essays and for himself, a book of appointments. He had put on weight. She took the book and tried to read it while he fulfilled his business engagements. At first she looked for an inscription but there was none. She found the essays mannered but the book itself, the giving of it, seemed momentous. She was vaguely disappointed by her own reaction to him after so long an absence, her slight criticism of his appearance, her impatience with his appointments, but there was no doubt all the same that she was happier and more alive than she had been since last she saw him. They dined together on several evenings and then he went home again. 'Take care of yourself,' he said, kissing her forehead; 'I'll see you soon.'

She lay down when he was gone and waited for the horror of loneliness to eat into her. Immediately she fell into a sleep of pleasant exhaustion and had a dream that she was fitting a dress to a fat client, sticking the pins straight into the cushioned flesh of this lady, who said: 'My dear, you have no idea how good that feels.' She woke feeling fit and hungry, took the dog for a long walk and noticed, avidly, the different shades of sky, the expressions on people's faces, the meditative vigil of cats and birds.

A week later the letter came. She spread it out on the table and let the words go to her head where they fitted like pieces in a puzzle, instantly familiar for she had written them herself, long ago and buried them there. She sipped at her coffee warily, like an old person, as though each parting of the lips might introduce a new sensation which would have to be coped with; and so it was. Everything was made new. 'Come home,' he wrote; 'I want to marry you.'

On the plane, on the way back to him, she closed her eyes and felt like a child that is being put to bed at the end of a birthday. All the treats and treasures of their first few months together crowded together in her drowsy head. It was extraordinary how, in the years she had waited for him, she never once thought of joy. She had forgotten that happiness is solid and sweet and juicy and that those who have it use it up and lick their fingers and never think that it might run out; and those who have not forget that it ever was.

Now memory tugged at her and dragged her giddily back; he sucked at her breast and her chin nested in his hair; she sat with her feet curled about the bar beneath the kitchen table while he made the breakfast coffee and talked to her over his shoulder; they met in a public place tantalizing each other with discreet half-accidental touches, bursting with their secrets, provocative to the poor unloved all around them; 'I love you,' he said.

'I love you.' Words sucked into the air out of her insecure centre, and from then on, forever, she could not stop saying them. Her smile severed her little allotment of window as she looked out at the foam of cloud on which the plane trustingly bounced along. Inevitably, this presumptuous pillaging of memory took her to the edge of the cliff, to the howling winds of pain and she hung on with her fingernails. It was all right now, he was waiting for her now. Would it be the same as it was, she wondered when she had recovered – the giddy, astounding joy? No, she thought, they were both older people; they would not spend so recklessly, but she thought it indulgently and without much regret.

It had been easy to put her own life in order. She gave her salon into the management of the excellent mousy girl who worked as her assistant and, partly in friendship and partly from anger, she handed over her little dog to the man who said she was in a cage. He had been wise and kind enough to offer his congratulations. Her only real doubt had been her flat. She had worked at it over ten years and she admired all its effects. She knew it would be unwise to impose her treasures in boxloads on someone who had already arranged his own home to his liking. She took some small paintings and a clock and put everything else into the hands of an estate agent. She had no regrets. She felt wonderfully light. Less nice, but more wonderful, she felt triumphant. She had come through. Like a saint who has rattled through the emptiness of a sinless life to emerge at death's end into a blaze of Glory, she exulted that her feet had not faltered.

The plane brought her back to land, but not to earth, and when she saw him waiting for her behind the barrier, she wanted to run into his arms, to feel the impact of his body, but she had to remind herself that his greetings had always been reserved. He had not seen her yet. He looked anxious. She watched his face and wanted only to please him. She still loved him. Even her feelings were true. She walked over to him quickly and touched his arm. He smiled. 'I'm glad you came,' he said; there was no doubting it.

When they entered his house she was confounded to find it quite unfamiliar. All had been changed. So often had she been forced to use these rooms as a setting for her fantasies, to face the fear of his friendship with other people, that she imagined they must be sealed and varnished over like a painting. 'Other women have lived here,' she thought immediately, noting frivolous curtains and ornaments and neurotic plants twisted in perplexity by their abandonment as she herself had once been: 'I don't know him.'

'Make yourself at home,' he said. 'It's your home now.'

She sat down to wrestle with her confusion. 'No,' she thought. 'You are my home.' His body issued no invitation. His arms did not enclose her like a home. She sat with her hands gripped between her knees as if she was depressed. It was the years, she told herself. They had wearied her. He bent down beside her and took her hands away from her. 'Are you all right?' She said nothing. She knew the temptation, when one has finally found, at a turning in the maze, the person who can lead one safely to its end, to lead them backward through the doors of one's past. She looked into his face and seeing concern there, she forgot. 'It's been a long journey,' she complained.

'You must sleep,' he said, thinking of taxis and planes. She allowed him to lead her to a little room with a single bed. 'Have a good rest,' he said and kissed her on the forehead.

When she woke it was morning and he was standing over her with a tray with tea. 'I shouldn't have woken you,' he said. 'I was excited, thinking of you here. Send me out if you want,' he added boldly, knowing she would not.

She sipped her tea. 'I want to watch you,' she said.

'Are you glad?' he said. 'Are you happy?'

She nodded cautiously.

'You were always on my mind, you know,' he said. 'You've known, haven't you, that I've always loved you.'

The phrases she had craved came tripping out in twos and threes. They brought no relief. All she felt was an unravelling, as if the defences she had built around herself were coming undone. 'Why?' she said, quietly, peevishly, to so many questions.

'I didn't know what to do.' He frowned in surprise at her demand. 'I know now. I want to marry you.'

She had not realized how much older she had grown. The cry of her own need, released with his summons, was ravenous. She needed his need. He had only to come and put his arms around her. 'How dare you,' she said, 'ask me to marry you without one single physical approach; no touch, no kiss, no gesture of affection? How terribly you presume.'

He looked appalled. His mouth opened but it was a while before he could make words. 'My dear,' he said. 'All that was so very long ago. I should have thought you understood. You've always understood. You were the one who understood.'

She felt her skin scraped by old black nails of fear. He sat on the edge of the bed. He too was afraid. 'A marriage,' he whispered. 'A marriage of the hearts.' He took her hand and it shocked her for it was the strongest physical communion they had made since her arrival.

'It has taken me so long to find out,' he said. 'And now I am so very sure.'

'You mean to live the rest of your life without physical love?' she said. 'You expect that of me? I am young. I want to love with my body.'

'No!' He was distressed by the things she said, exasperated by her obtuseness. 'Of course you will have lovers. I won't mind. I won't ask. And I ... It will be no different, except that we will have each other for life. I will make sure that you are protected. You won't be hurt. You won't even know.'

She thought afterwards that she must have left the bed, got out of the room, like a snake. With a hiss and a lightning slither, she was gone from him. She had no memory of walking or running down the stairs, of throwing things in cases and snapping them shut. All she could properly recall was standing in the hall with her cases, waiting for a taxi, and the hardness of her face in the hall mirror.

Then beside her reflection was his face, full of misery and terror, full of shadows as though he was being wiped out.

'I live, you see,' he was explaining, 'on romance. I cannot live without it. I am fuelled by it. It does not make me happy. I am very lonely. I simply live on it as you live on air. I think no more of it than you think of air.'

She heard a car pulling up outside and ran into the street. 'Airport,' she said to the taxi driver. She flung her cases into the car, scrambling after them, feeling the thumping of her heart echoed in bright, burning discs behind her closed eyelids.

'Are you all right?' the driver said as they bumped along.

'Yes,' she said in surprise. She did not feel anything, no grief, no disappointment, just the vague tremor of emergence from a nightmare. She no longer felt, as she used to, that her separation from him was an amputation. He had established himself as a separate person, quite irreconcilable to her heartfelt self and now, she thought with shaky surprise, I am free.

'Free.' She was back in a plane wrapped in many thicknesses of sky, beginning, boldly, to conceive of a life of her own. She sipped her drink. 'Free as a bird.' The phrase made her think of her dogminding friend and she considered how she might telephone him and ask him to take her to dinner and then she would bring him back to her bed. The solidness of ordinary material things comforted her mind as images of love had done yesterday. 'Now,' she thought, 'I will begin to be selfish. I will do what other people do. I will make myself a life.' She proceeded to invent for herself an itinerary of mandatory pleasure. A weekend in the country with a man who liked wine and lovemaking. A new car. A holiday in the sun with a girlfriend. Now and again there intruded on these substantial images some alternative, shadowy vision and she pushed it out.

She thought of fur coats, of paintings, of the Fortuny dress a woman friend had offered to sell her. The image slid hopefully back. It was his face. 'No.' She was firm; 'I have freed myself.' Curiosity compelled her to peek again and now she could not look away. It was not the face that had cut into her with pain in all the years they had been apart; his smiling face that she had looked on and loved, without which she could not live. It was a face full of misery and terror, full of shadows, an image trapped in the frame of a mirror, the face of a man cut off from hope; the face of a creature in a cage.

Cruise boats, jewels. She heaped up the edges of her mind.

She longed for the journey to be over so that she could fill up her life with physical things, dazzle her mind with their venality so as to shut out all emotion forever, but she was in the air and his face was still there. It was finding a voice. 'Free me.' 'No.' She was horrified. 'It is I who have been held.' His face pulled at her and tears filled her eyes. Free me. The shadow settled into her patiently.

She knew, had known all along what she had done. She had shut him in. She had taken his freedom when she claimed her own. 'Why me?' she asked as human beings always do but she knew the answer to that too. It was because she loved him. What he was and how he was; both would be her concern for as long as she lived.

She telephoned him from the airport. 'I've been thinking,' she said. 'I needed time to think.' She had considered his strange proposal. Reduced to proportion it was much the same as every lover's pledge to another: 'I need you.' She knew that the need would go on and on. It was what she wanted, if not what she desired. Her own life would not alter much.

She would have no less of him than before, and a little more. Who knew how the years would alter things. Who ever knew.

'And . . . ?' his voice across the channel sounded subdued.

'I'm coming home,' she said quickly.

'Oh, yes,' he said and she could tell from his altered tone that he was smiling.

All the way back she held on to his smile as a child who

is displaced and weary holds on to a cloth bear or a doll and then when she saw him again she realized that she no longer feared him, that for the first time in the years she had known him they had made a relationship and without thinking she put her arms around him and he held on to her.

MORE ABOUT PENGUINS, PELICANS
AND PUFFINS

For further information about books available from Penguins please write to Dept EP, Penguin Books Ltd, Harmondsworth, Middlesex UB7 0DA.

In the U.S.A.: For a complete list of books available from Penguins in the United States write to Dept DG, Penguin Books, 299 Murray Hill Parkway, East Rutherford, New Jersey 07073.

In Canada: For a complete list of books available from Penguins in Canada write to Penguin Books Canada Ltd, 2801 John Street, Markham, Ontario L3R 1B4.

In Australia: For a complete list of books available from Penguins in Australia write to the Marketing Department, Penguin Books Australia Ltd, P.O. Box 257, Ringwood, Victoria 3134.

In New Zealand: For a complete list of books available from Penguins in New Zealand write to the Marketing Department, Penguin Books (N.Z.) Ltd, Private Bag, Takapuna, Auckland 9.

In India: For a complete list of books available from Penguins in India write to Penguin Overseas Ltd, 706 Eros Apartments, 56 Nehru Place, New Delhi 110019.

A CHOICE OF PENGUINS

☐ **Monsignor Quixote** Graham Greene £1.95

'Greene's best, most absorbing, adept and effortless novel', as the *Spectator* described it, circulates around the shrines and fleshpots of Spain, with an endearing, modern-day Don Quixote and his unlikely travelling companion, a deposed communist mayor. 'A deliciously funny novel' – *The Times*

☐ **The Philosopher's Pupil** Iris Murdoch £2.50

'We are back, of course, with great delight, in the land of Iris Murdoch, which is like no other but Prospero's . . .' – *Sunday Telegraph*. And, as expected, her new masterpiece is 'marvellous . . . compulsive reading, hugely funny' – *Spectator*

☐ **The Orlando Trilogy** Isabel Colegate £3.95

Orlando King's rise to success, amid the gaiety and splintering ideals of the thirties and forties, is charted in this compelling family saga by the award-winning author of *The Shooting Party*. 'Tender, intelligent . . . highly recommended' – *Guardian*

☐ **White Mischief** James Fox £1.95

Who did kill the 22nd Earl of Erroll in Nairobi? The bestselling reconstruction of 'one of the most fascinating and intriguing cases of this century . . . Eccentric settlers and shady aristos, neurotic wives and lounge-lizards. The cast and setting are unique' – William Boyd. 'Marvellously entertaining' – Auberon Waugh

☐ **The Penguin Collected Stories of Isaac Bashevis Singer** £4.95

Forty-seven unforgettable tales of Jewish faith, magic and exile. 'Never was the Nobel Prize more deserved . . . He belongs with the giants' – *Sunday Times*

☐ **Holy Pictures** Clare Boylan £1.95

The beautifully drawn comedy of a young girl's awakening to adolescence in the Dublin of 1925. 'Sharp as a serpent's tooth . . . it is a very long time since a first novel of such fun and wit and style has come so confidently out of Ireland' – William Trevor

A CHOICE OF PENGUINS

☐ *Scandal* **A. N. Wilson** £1.95

Sexual peccadillos, treason and blackmail are all ingredients on the boil in A. N. Wilson's new, *cordon noir* comedy. 'Drily witty, deliciously nasty' – *Sunday Telegraph*

☐ *The Sword of Honour Trilogy* **Evelyn Waugh** £3.95

Containing *Men at Arms*, *Officers and Gentlemen* and *Unconditional Surrender*, the trilogy described by Cyril Connolly as 'unquestionably the finest novels to have come out of the war'.

☐ *The Alexander Trilogy* **Mary Renault** £4.95

Containing *Fire from Heaven*, *The Persian Boy* and *Funeral Games* – her re-creation of Ancient Greece acclaimed by Gore Vidal as 'one of this century's most unexpectedly original works of art'.

These books should be available at all good bookshops or newsagents, but if you live in the UK or the Republic of Ireland and have difficulty in getting to a bookshop, they can be ordered by post. Please indicate the titles required and fill in the form below.

NAME _____ BLOCK CAPITALS

ADDRESS _____

_____

_____

Enclose a cheque or postal order payable to The Penguin Bookshop to cover the total price of books ordered, plus 50p for postage. Readers in the Republic of Ireland should send £IR equivalent to the sterling prices, plus 67p for postage. Send to: The Penguin Bookshop, 54/56 Bridlesmith Gate, Nottingham, NG1 2GP.

You can also order by phoning (0602) 599295, and quoting your Barclaycard or Access number.

Every effort is made to ensure the accuracy of the price and availability of books at the time of going to press, but it is sometimes necessary to increase prices and in these circumstances retail prices may be shown on the covers of books which may differ from the prices shown in this list or elsewhere. This list is not an offer to supply any book.

This order service is only available to residents in the UK and the Republic of Ireland.